THE AFTER
SCHOOL
DETECTIVE
CLUB

THE CASE OF THE DASTARDLY DOGNAPPERS

Mark Dawson

WRITING WITH ALLAN BOROUGHS

ILLUSTRATED BY BEN MANTLE

WELBECK
FLAME

Published in 2023 by Welbeck Flame
An imprint of Welbeck Children's Limited,
part of Welbeck Publishing Group.
Offices in: London - 20 Mortimer Street, London W1T 3JW &
Sydney - Level 17, 207 Kent St, Sydney NSW 2000 Australia
www.welbeckpublishing.com

A CIP catalogue record for this book is available from the British Library.

ISBN: 978 1 80130 083 4

Printed and bound by CPI Group (UK)

10 9 8 7 6 5 4 3 2 1

To My Family

Lucy

Brave, loyal and athletic. She wants to be
an Olympian so don't get in her way . . .

Max

The geek with a wicked sense of humour.

Self-styled child genius – just don't tell his mum.

Joe

Adventurous, funny and a great cook – but
don't believe everything he says.

Charlie

Fierce as a lion, she loves her dog Sherlock more

than people. Don't ever call her Charlotte!

Sherlock

Loud bark, cold nose,

big heart – the fifth

member of the club.

1

THE DINNER PARTY

Joe was arguing with his mother, and it was not going well.

'I've already told you, Mum,' he said. 'It's a matter of life and death.'

Penelope Carter rolled her eyes with the weary expression of someone who has more important things to do than listen to a matter of life and death. 'All you've told me,' she said, as she tied a kitchen apron around her waist, 'is that you have to go to the school sports ground. It's a Saturday, Joe. Surely, it can't be that important?'

Joe took a deep breath and blew it out slowly. 'It's like I said,' he explained, as calmly as he could manage. 'Lucy's running in an important race today and I'm meeting the others so we can cheer her on.'

'Well, there you are then,' said his mother, selecting a knife from the wooden block on the kitchen counter. 'Lucy Yeung spends her whole life running races. She's bound to win; she always does. So why do you have to be there?'

'Because it's what friends do, Mum,' said Joe. 'This race is important for Lucy. If she wins, she'll get to try out for the county athletics squad. I *have* to be there.'

Penelope Carter took a heavy package from the fridge and began to unwrap it. 'As I explained to you, Joseph, I have *very* important clients coming for dinner tonight and I need you to be here.'

Joe's mother had started a new job, working for an estate agent in the town, which, she explained, meant that she had to 'show houses' to her clients. Joe couldn't imagine why someone had

to be shown a house. In his experience, houses generally stayed in one place, and they had addresses so that people could find them easily. Showing people where they were didn't sound like much of a job.

When he pointed this out to his mother, she had become quite annoyed. 'It's not like that, Joe,' she had said, in one of her 'you wouldn't understand' voices. 'The job of an estate agent is very skilled. It's about matching the right sort of people with their ideal property. My clients are people of taste and refinement.'

His mother finished unwrapping the package and studied the contents carefully. Joe looked over her shoulder then recoiled quickly. The package appeared to contain a large blob of slime with tentacles.

'What is *that?*' he said, wrinkling his nose.

'Fresh octopus,' said his mother, as though this was obvious. 'I'm making a seafood stew with a herb salad. It will be lovely.'

Joe stared at the octopus and thought that the last thing it looked was 'lovely'. If this was what people with 'taste and refinement' ate, then he was pretty sure he didn't want to spend an evening with them.

'Are you *sure* you want me there?' he said. 'I mean, I wouldn't want to get in the way of that whole "matching people with their ideal property" thing.'

His mother gave him a stern look. 'Oh no you don't, my lad. My clients are extremely important people. Lord and Lady Fitchwitherington are practically related to royalty and tonight they're coming here for dinner and they're bringing their daughter with them. So, I need you to be here.'

Joe sighed. He knew better than to argue with his mother, but there were other ways to get out of the dinner party. If he promised to be back on time, he could always claim later that he'd missed his bus or forgotten the way home.

'Okay, Mum,' he said, putting on his most sincere smile. 'I'll just pop out for a little while to cheer for Lucy and then I'll be straight back in time for dinner. How's that?'

Penelope Carter fixed her son with the sort of glare that had been known to reduce shop assistants to jelly. 'You'd better be, my lad,' she said, wagging a finger in his direction. 'I want my clients

5

to see that we have a happy and stable home life. So, if you're not back here being happy and stable all evening then you will be spending the rest of half-term confined to your bedroom.'

2

WINNER AND LOSERS

'All I'm saying is that you should try coming bird-spotting with me and Sherlock,' said Charlie. 'You might learn something.'

Max looked up from the thick book he was reading and took a leisurely bite from the cloud of pink candy floss he held in his free hand. 'I spot birds all the time, Charlie,' he said. 'They've got wings and feathers. What else do I need to know about them?'

'It's not just about spotting them,' said Charlie. 'It's the whole experience of being outside in the fresh air and getting some exercise.'

'I get plenty of exercise, thanks,' said Max with a sniff. 'I'll have you know I'm very sporty.'

'You? Sporty?'

'Sure,' said Max. 'I could watch sport for hours. Why else would I be here on school sports day?'

Max and Charlie sat in the top row of seats of the small grandstand that overlooked the school playing fields, with Sherlock perched on the seat between them. The grandstand was busy with students from St Enid's, chatting excitedly and waving their school scarves as they waited for the races to begin.

While Max returned to his book, Charlie took in the scene. Competitors wearing shorts and singlets were scattered around the field in the spring sunshine. They sprinted along the track, leaped into the long-jump pit and jumped over tall bars while Mr Finnegan, the games teacher, blew on his whistle until his face had turned the same shade of red as his tracksuit.

Charlie looked at Max, who was absorbed in his book again. 'Honestly, Max,' she said.

'There's no point being here to support Lucy if you're just going to read a book the whole time. What are you reading anyway?'

Max looked up. *'The Adventures of Sherlock Holmes,'* he said with a grin. 'No, not you, Sherlock.' At the mention of his name, the little dog had jumped up and wagged his tail enthusiastically. *'This* Sherlock was a famous detective that lived in Victorian times. He was brilliant. He could tell all sorts of things about people just by looking at them and picking up clues about their lives. I'm reading it because I think it will make me a better detective.'

Charlie frowned. 'Well, I think putting it down and supporting Lucy would make you a better friend,' she said.

Max reluctantly closed the book and tucked it into his backpack. 'When is Lucy's race anyway?' he said. 'Have I got time to get some more candy floss from the ice cream van?'

'I think you've had enough,' said Charlie.

'And Sherlock's had more than enough. If my dog gets fat, I shall blame you. Besides, it looks like the race is about to start, look.'

On the field in front of the grandstand, several young athletes were performing their warm-up exercises. Mr Finnegan was measuring the distance between the freshly painted running lanes and writing things down on the clipboard he carried with him.

'Remind me how far she has to run?' said Max.

'Eight hundred metres,' said Charlie. 'It's her best event.'

'That's about seven hundred and ninety metres further than anyone should have to run,' said Max, taking another bite of candy floss.

'Lucy told me her personal best time is two minutes and eighteen seconds,' said Charlie. 'That's faster than anyone else at the school.'

Max watched the runners gather at the starting line. 'I recognise most of them,' he said. 'But who's that?'

He pointed to a tall girl with long blonde hair who stood by herself, stretching out her long limbs. Her brow was furrowed in concentration and she looked extremely serious.

'I think she's a new girl,' said Charlie. 'I heard her family have just arrived, but she's not in any of my classes.'

Max shrugged. 'It doesn't matter,' he said breezily. 'Lucy's going to win by a mile. Then we can go and get some ice creams to celebrate.'

Sherlock jumped up in his seat and gave a sudden bark. They turned to see Joe grinning and waving as he made his way along the row of seats towards them.

'Sorry I'm late,' he gasped as he patted Sherlock and sat down.

'Ah-ha!' said Max suddenly. 'Using my superior powers of deductive reasoning, I can tell that the reason you're late is that you overslept this morning and had to get here on your bicycle.'

'He's reading Sherlock Holmes,' said Charlie by

way of an explanation. 'He thinks it will make him a better detective.'

'That's amazing, Max,' said Joe. 'How did you guess all that?'

'Elementary, my dear Joseph,' said Max. 'First of all, I noticed that you haven't combed your hair, which tells me you got ready in a hurry this morning. Then I saw that you are red in the face, which shows that you have been exerting yourself. Therefore, I deduced that you got up late and hurried here on your bicycle.' He breathed on his fingernails and polished them on his lapel.

'What's so amazing,' said Joe, 'is how you managed to be so completely wrong about everything. Firstly, I never comb my hair when I get up, it just wastes time. Second, I had to get up early this morning to go shopping with my mum because she's having a dinner party. And lastly, when I did get out of the house, I had to run for the bus.'

'Oh,' said Max, looking crestfallen. 'I guess my

powers of deduction need a little work.' Then he brightened. 'So, your mum's having a dinner party? What's she cooking?'

'Don't ask,' said Joe. 'I'm not sure it's entirely dead yet. I haven't missed the race, have I?'

'It's about to start,' said Charlie. 'Look, there's Lucy now.'

On the other side of the playing field, Lucy came out of the sports hall in her running kit, looking very serious. She was accompanied by her father, who had an arm around her shoulders and was talking earnestly in her ear.

'It looks like her dad is giving her some last minute tips,' said Joe. They all knew that he took personal charge of Lucy's training.

Max cupped his hands to his mouth. 'Hey, Luce!' he yelled. 'Up here!'

Lucy looked up and saw her friends sitting in the grandstand. She broke into a smile and waved as they all jumped up and down and Sherlock barked.

'Good luck!' yelled Charlie.

'Knock 'em dead, Lucy,' shouted Joe.

* * *

Down on the field, Lucy gave her friends a last wave and turned back to her dad. Ken Yeung frowned. 'Now is not the time to be distracted by your friends, Lucy.'

'I know, Dad. Don't worry, I know what I need to do.'

'Stay focused,' he said. 'You've trained hard for this day, and nothing can stop you as long as you concentrate.'

'I will,' she said. 'Trust me. I know I can win this race.'

Ken Yeung gave his daughter a hug then retreated to the sidelines to stand with the other parents. Lucy put down her towel and her water bottle and took her place on the starting line.

She looked along the running track and tried to visualise herself running the race the way her father had taught her. Then she smiled to herself.

Once she had won this race, she would be on her way to becoming a world-class athlete.

She noticed that the girl in the next lane was someone she didn't know. She was very tall, even taller than Lucy, and she had the long, muscular limbs of an athlete. Her blonde hair was tied back in a ponytail and she wore a deep frown. Lucy supposed she must be new in the school.

'Hi there,' said Lucy, giving her a smile. 'Good luck in the race.'

The girl turned and glared at Lucy with her cold blue eyes. 'I don't need luck to beat you,' she said unpleasantly. 'I've got talent.'

Lucy was so taken aback that her mouth dropped open. Before she could reply, the girl had turned away and crouched down in preparation for the start. Lucy was about to tell the girl how rude she thought she was when Mr Finnegan took up his position beside the starting line with a megaphone in his hand.

The megaphone screeched like a cat in pain

when he turned it on, and he had to bang it with his fist before it stopped. 'Now pay attention, you lot,' he barked. 'This is the final of the eight hundred metres, which is two laps of the playing field. And I'm sure I don't need to remind you' – he glanced at Lucy – 'that the winner will get the chance to run in the county championships. Good luck, everyone.'

Lucy took up position and tried to put the other girl's rudeness out of her mind as she focused on the race. She crouched down with her legs braced and her fingers just touching the start line as she had been taught.

Mr Finnegan pulled a small starting pistol from his pocket. 'On your marks,' he called out dramatically. 'Get set...' There was a short pause, followed by the sharp crack of the pistol.

Lucy launched herself forwards with a powerful leap and began pumping her legs. Almost immediately her pre-race nerves dropped away as she fell into her stride and found her natural running rhythm.

She got a good start and quickly pulled away from the rest of the pack. She could hear her father's voice telling her to run the first two hundred metres as fast as possible. *Get ahead of the others early on*, he would say. *Don't get boxed in by the other runners.*

As she neared the end of the first lap, she threw

a quick glance over her shoulder. The rest of the pack were a good twenty metres behind her, and it looked like most of them were already tired. That was good, she thought, she was nearly there.

She focused on keeping a good pace as she entered the last lap, feeling her muscles burn as they began to tire. *Now is the time to push, Lucy,* she heard her dad's voice say. *Now is the time to show them what you are made of.*

She could see the finish line now. Mr Finnegan and another teacher had stretched a ribbon across the track, and he was holding the stopwatch in his other hand. She gritted her teeth as she rounded the final bend and put her head down to sprint for the line. Somewhere up in the stands she could hear her friends shouting and Sherlock's excited bark. She was going to win.

And then someone pulled level with her. She glanced sideways and saw the new girl running alongside her with a relaxed style that looked smooth and effortless. Lucy forced herself to run faster, pounding the track hard as she tried to pick up more speed. But no matter how hard Lucy tried, the other girl stayed with her. They were into the last thirty metres now, twenty, fifteen.

And then it happened.

Barely ten metres from the finish line, the other girl pulled ahead effortlessly, almost as though Lucy was standing still. Lucy felt the fight going out of her. She tried to claw her way back over the last couple of metres, ducking her head towards the tape as her dad had taught her. But it was no use.

She crossed the line a metre behind the other girl. Her legs immediately buckled and she collapsed onto her hands and knees. The other girl stood a few metres away with her hands on her hips as though she was hardly out of breath.

Lucy looked around and saw her friends up in the grandstand. Charlie, Max and Joe had all fallen silent and were just staring and even Sherlock had gone quiet. Then she saw her dad, standing on the sidelines, and Lucy thought the look of disappointment on his face was more than she could bear.

She climbed painfully to her feet and brushed the dirt from her knees. She couldn't understand how this had happened. She had always been the fastest in their school and she had been the favourite to win the race. Who was this girl that had beaten her so easily?

She picked up her towel and bottle and took a large drink of water. Then she remembered one other lesson her dad had taught her. *Whatever else happens on the track,* he had said, *it's important to show good sportsmanship at all times.*

However disappointed she was, Lucy knew what she had to do now. She walked across the track to where the new girl was standing. 'You ran really well,' said Lucy. 'Congratulations.' She forced herself to give the girl a smile and held out her hand.

The other girl looked at Lucy coldly and her lip

curled. 'Why on earth would I want to shake hands with a loser?' she said. 'It might rub off on me.'

Lucy's jaw dropped open. She had put down the girl's earlier rudeness to nerves, but this was too much. 'Wait a minute,' she said crossly. 'Just because you won the race doesn't mean you can talk to me like that.'

The girl was laughing openly now. 'Sure it does,' she said. 'Winners get to do anything they want. And as for losers... well, you know what they say. Once a loser, always a loser.'

And with that, she turned on her heel and strode away, leaving Lucy staring after her.

3

THE THUNDERER

'She said *what* to you?' Charlie stared at Lucy with a furious expression and even Sherlock let out a little growl as he sat by her side.

'I know,' said Lucy. 'It's unbelievable, isn't it? All I did was congratulate her on winning.'

The gang sat glumly around the table in the beach hut, sympathising with Lucy after the loss of her race. 'She's got to be the rudest person I've ever heard of,' said Joe. 'You'd think she'd be a bit nicer after she won the race.'

'Well, statistically speaking,' said Max, through a mouthful of chocolate biscuits, 'serious athletes tend to be more aggressive than other people.

It's what makes them competitive.'

Charlie shot Max a warning look. 'Not helping, Max,' she hissed.

'No, he could be right,' said Lucy. 'Maybe that's my problem. I'm just too nice to people. Perhaps I'm not really cut out to be an athlete after all.'

'That's nonsense, Lucy,' said Joe at once. 'No one runs faster than you do. You're going to be an Olympic gold medallist one day; I just know it.' The others all agreed enthusiastically. Sherlock jumped up on the sofa to lick Lucy's face and took the opportunity to snaffle a mouthful of ginger biscuits from the table at the same time.

Lucy smiled gratefully at her friends but still managed to look really sad at the same time. 'Thanks guys,' she said. 'I guess I'll just have to get used to the idea that I don't win everything any more.'

'Well, at least we've got half-term to look forward to,' said Charlie. 'So, what shall we do next week?'

'I think my week is going to be taken up with

more training runs,' said Lucy. 'After the race, my dad said I'm going to have to work much harder. I think he's planning to have me running five miles a day for the whole week.'

'And my mum seems to have a whole week planned around her new clients, Lord and Lady Fitchwitherington,' said Joe. 'Apparently, they're "people of taste and refinement".'

'It makes them sound like chocolate bars,' said Max, wistfully. 'Well, I don't think I'm in for much fun this holiday either. Mum's been very worried about my grades since I got one hundred per cent in my science exam.'

'Why is she worried if you got one hundred per cent?' said Lucy. 'I would have thought she'd be really pleased.'

'According to Mum, it means I'm in danger of letting my guard down,' said Max. *'You get one hundred per cent, and you think you can start to relax, Maximillian,'* said Max, doing quite a good impression of his mother. *'Then the next time you only get ninety-nine per cent and it's all downhill from there.'* They all laughed.

'It's no joking matter,' said Max. 'She's got extra lessons planned for me all next week and I can't go out until I've finished them. If I get less than a hundred per cent next time, I'll never see daylight again!'

'This is no good,' said Lucy, standing up suddenly. 'We can't sit around being glum all week. How about we go down to the pier for an ice cream? My treat... to celebrate being such a loser,' she added with a smile.

Sherlock woofed delightedly. 'Ice cream' was one of the words he understood very well, along with 'sausages', 'walk' and 'seagull'. He bounded off the sofa and ran around the hut in excited circles as the others began to gather their things.

When Joe had locked the door, they set out along the seafront in the direction of the pier. The day was crisp, but the sun shone brightly with a promise of the summer to come, and pretty soon they were all smiling because there is nothing like being out with your best friends on a sunny day.

They stopped at the end of the pier and Lucy bought them all ice creams, with a stick of flaky chocolate plus a small cone for Sherlock. Charlie held it out for him to take a lick and he promptly snapped his jaws shut over the entire cone.

'I don't think Sherlock understands the idea of an ice cream cone,' said Max as they continued their walk. 'It never lasts him more than about four seconds.'

'That's because he thinks if he finishes it quickly, he can have some of ours,' said Joe.

'Well, he's not wrong, is he?' said Lucy, looking at Charlie, who was in the process of breaking off a piece of her own ice cream cone to give to Sherlock.

Their laughter was interrupted by the sound of an engine revving loudly behind them. They turned in time to see a black van zoom past, sending up a small cloud of dust and stones. Its tyres squealed as it turned a corner and disappeared from view.

'He was going way too fast,' said Lucy with a frown.

'I've never seen that van before,' said Charlie, finishing the last of her ice cream. 'Maybe it's from out of town.'

Max stroked his chin and raised an eyebrow. 'Interesting,' he said mysteriously. 'A van we've never seen before. It could be an important clue.'

'And it could be just a van,' said Charlie. 'Honestly, Max, since you've been reading Sherlock Holmes, you think everything's a clue.'

'Everything *is* a clue,' insisted Max. 'You just have to work out what it's a clue to.'

'Speaking of things we've never seen before,' said Joe. 'What is *that*?'

They turned to look, and everybody gasped at the sight that was rumbling along the street towards them.

It was a very large motorbike, painted green, with shiny chrome wheels and an enormous headlamp. What made the machine so unusual was the gleaming, bullet-shaped carriage attached to one side of it. The carriage ran on two wheels and it had brown leather seats that had been polished to a deep shine.

'It's a motorcycle and sidecar!' said Joe excitedly. 'I remember my grandad telling me about them. Lots of people used to have them if they couldn't afford a car.'

Almost as strange as the motorcycle was the person riding it. The rider wore a long leather coat, split down the back so that it rested either side of the bike. He had on long leather boots, long gauntlets and a leather half-helmet with separate goggles.

The rider raised a hand in greeting and slowed down to pull in to the side of the road. As he drew closer, they saw his thick, bushy beard and sparkling blue eyes behind his goggles. 'It's Captain Tom!' said Joe excitedly.

The children had met Captain Tom the previous Christmas when he had helped them to catch the gang of smugglers that had been working along the coast. They all liked the old lighthouse keeper immensely but none of them had any idea that he owned a motorcycle.

'Well, hello there!' declared Captain Tom as the motorbike stuttered to a stop. He pushed up his goggles and grinned at them. 'Beautiful day, don't you think?'

'Captain Tom!' chorused all the children together.

'It's lovely to see you again,' said Lucy.

'What a fantastic motorbike!' said Joe, reaching out and running his fingers along the smooth green paintwork. 'Have you just bought it?'

'Dear me, no.' Captain Tom laughed. 'I bought *The Thunderer* back in 1965 when I had my first job. I've kept it in working order ever since.' He looked up at the sky. 'But I only ever bring the old girl out on sunny days,' he added.

'1965?' said Joe. 'That's...' He began to count up on his fingers but quickly gave up. 'A *really* long time ago,' he said eventually.

'Where are you going with it?' said Lucy.

'Well, it's such a lovely day, I thought I'd take a run up the coast and take Pugly for a walk at the nature reserve.'

For the first time, they noticed that Captain Tom was not alone. Sitting in the sidecar was a small black and brown dog. Pugly was not a handsome dog by any stretch of the imagination. He had short legs and a fat little body and his nose was all squashed up. His brow was wrinkled as though he was permanently worried and, strangest of all, his bulbous brown eyes seemed to point in different directions.

Pugly put his paws up on the edge of the sidecar to greet the children and Sherlock barked excitedly when he saw him. Over the last few months, Sherlock and Pugly had become firm friends when they had met on their walks.

'Well, it's a lovely day for a drive,' said Lucy, after they had made a fuss of Pugly.

'And Pugly will enjoy the nature reserve,' said Charlie. 'Me and Sherlock go there sometimes. It makes a nice change.'

'Oh, it's a change alright,' said the captain, stroking his beard. 'But that's not why I'm taking him up there.'

'Then, why are you taking him?' said Max.

'Haven't you heard?' said Captain Tom. He glanced up and down the road suspiciously, as though he was afraid that someone might overhear them. Then he leaned towards the children and lowered his voice dramatically. 'There's *dognappers* about.'

'Dognappers?' The children blinked at the old man, confused.

'What are dognappers?' said Lucy.

'Thieves and rascals is what they are,' said Captain Tom with a scowl. 'They steal dogs from ordinary folk like you and me, then they sell them to other people who are looking for a pet of their own.'

'They steal dogs?' gasped Charlie. She crouched down and pulled Sherlock closer to her. 'Surely no one would do that around here?'

'That's where you're wrong, young Charlie,' said Captain Tom. 'I heard two dogs went missing from Walberswick last week. And only this morning I heard that Cornelia Jobsworthy lost her little Pekingese while she was taking her for a walk. She said she only took her eyes off her for a moment.'

'That's terrible,' said Lucy. 'Mrs Jobsworthy is the mayor, isn't she?'

'She certainly is,' said Captain Tom. 'I'm thinking

if the Mayor of Southwold can get her dog stolen then anyone can. That's why I'm taking no chances with Pugly.'

'Do the police have any clues?' said Max.

Captain Tom shook his head gravely. 'They think it must be an organised gang,' he said. 'They probably grab the dog and bundle it into a van before the owner even notices they're gone.'

'A van?' said Max thoughtfully.

'Anyhow, I can't stay here chatting all day,' said Captain Tom. 'Pugly needs his walk.' He stamped down on the old bike's kick-starter and *The Thunderer* roared to life in a cloud of blue smoke that left them all coughing.

'Take care now,' he shouted over the noise of the engine as he lowered his goggles. 'And mind you keep a close watch on young Sherlock,' he said to Charlie. 'Can't be too careful with dognappers about.'

And with that, Captain Tom revved the engine and *The Thunderer* roared away in a fog of exhaust fumes with Pugly looking out over the back seat. 'What an awful story,' said Lucy. 'I can't believe anyone would do such a horrible thing as to steal someone's dog.'

Charlie took Sherlock's lead from her pocket and clipped it to his collar. 'I feel better if I'm holding on to him,' she said when she saw the others looking at her. 'I couldn't bear the thought of someone taking him away from me.'

'We won't let anyone take Sherlock away,' said Joe. 'He's part of the After-School Detective Club and we all stick together.'

'Totally,' said Max. 'Besides, those dognappers have probably moved on by now. We won't hear any more about them.'

'Thanks,' said Charlie. 'But if you don't mind, I'm going to take Sherlock home. I don't like the idea of being out with him after dark.' She turned and headed back along the promenade in the direction of her house, walking quickly with Sherlock trotting along behind.

'Poor Charlie,' said Lucy. 'She seems really worried about the dognappers.'

'I'm sure there's nothing to worry about,' said Max. He looked at his watch. 'She was right about one thing, though: it will be getting dark soon. I'd better be getting home for dinner.'

'Dinner!' cried Joe suddenly. He slapped his hand against his forehead. 'I'm such an idiot. I completely forgot; Mum's important clients are coming for dinner tonight. She said she'd kill me if I wasn't there on time.' Before Max or Lucy could say anything, Joe turned and sprinted away along the street.

'I suppose I'd better get home too,' said Lucy forlornly. 'I just know Dad's going to insist I go out for a training run tonight. Come on, I'll walk with you as far as your house.'

As they started along the street, Max gave Lucy a sympathetic glance. 'I really am sorry about your race, Luce,' he said. 'What with that and the dognappers, it's been a pretty miserable

Saturday in Southwold.'

Lucy shrugged. 'Oh, I don't mind about the race too much,' she said. 'All athletes lose races at some time or another. But that horrible, rude girl really got to me. I'd really like to give her a piece of my mind.' She frowned. 'I just wish I knew who she was.'

4

THE DINNER
FROM HELL

Joe sprinted all the way home, hoping that it was not as late as his watch told him it was. He avoided the front door and went around the back of the house, hoping to slip in unnoticed. If he was lucky, he might be able to sneak upstairs and then pretend he'd been home for ages, studying quietly in his room.

It was a good plan, and it went wrong almost immediately.

Penelope Carter was in the kitchen, red-faced and harried. Her hair was limp from the cooking steam, and she had a large splash of red sauce down the front of her shirt. Several pots boiled and rattled on the stovetop and the washing-up was piled high in the sink.

'Joseph Carter, what time do you call *this*?' yelled his mother as he came through the door. 'There are a million things left to do, our guests are due in less than fifteen minutes, and I still need to get dressed and do my hair. And now you saunter in here an hour late as though there was nothing important happening this evening.'

Joe gave his mother what he hoped was a disarming smile. 'Sorry, Mum,' he said bashfully. 'It's just that we were on our way to buy ice creams and I was going to come home straight after that, but then we met Captain Tom and he's got a really cool old motorbike called *The Thunderer* and he told us that apparently there are dognappers in Southwold and what they do is, they steal people's dogs and then they—'

'Be *quiet*, Joseph!' yelled his mother. 'I do not need to know about dognippers right now.'

'It's dognappers, Mum,' said Joe quickly.

'What I do need,' said his mother loudly, 'is some help to entertain our guests this evening. Do you appreciate how important it could be to have somebody like Lord Fitchwitherington as a family friend?'

Joe was thoughtful. 'I dunno,' he said. 'Could he... make me a knight or something?'

'No, he couldn't make you a knight,' snapped his mother. 'Only the king can do that. But what he can do is introduce us to the right people. If we start moving in the same circles as nobility, I could be selling houses for all the best people in the country. So, I need you on your best behaviour tonight, young man, or you will not be going out to see those frightful friends of yours for the rest of the holidays. Do you understand me?'

Joe was quite used to the idea that his mother did not approve of his friends but the thought of being banned from seeing them was more than he could bear. So, he nodded and said, 'Yes, Mum,' as apologetically as he could manage.

'Good,' said his mother. 'Now, I am going upstairs to get ready, and you are going to help your father lay the table. And remember what I said: I want nothing but charm and politeness from you all evening, *or else.*'

Joe found his father in the dining room, uncorking the wine and sniffing the bottle. Mike Carter always chose the wine when they had guests and he liked to think of himself as something of an expert. 'I've been saving this for an important occasion,' he said, as Joe came in. He held up the bottle to the light and squinted at it, though Joe had no idea what he might be looking for. 'I think this will impress His Lordship.'

Joe started laying the table and thought about something that had been bothering him. 'Dad?' he said eventually. 'What do lords and ladies actually look like?'

Mike Carter looked up from the wine bottle. 'Eh? Well, they look like everyone else, I suppose.'

'No, I mean do they wear crowns and ermine robes and stuff?'

'No, of course not,' said his dad. 'Well, not when they come to dinner anyway. At least... I hope they don't.' A worried frown creased his face as though this was a possibility he had not considered.

'Well, am I meant to curtsey or something when I meet them?'

Mike Carter gave his son a baffled look. 'Curtseying is what women do, Joe,' he said. 'And besides, that's just for the king. I think you just say, "How are you?", the same as you would to anyone else. They'll probably be very normal people.'

Joe was puzzled. 'But, what I don't understand is... if they look the same as everyone else, and they don't dress any differently and you don't have to curtsey to them, then how do we know that they're a real lord and lady?'

'Eh?' Mike Carter frowned. 'Well... I, er, expect they... I mean they probably...' He paused and scratched his head. 'Well, you just have to take it on trust, Joe. Important people don't go around lying about that sort of thing.'

Joe was ready to ask more questions but, fortunately for his dad, they were interrupted by a loud scream from upstairs. 'Oh, my heavens, they're early,' cried Penelope Carter. 'Mike, they're here already. Do something!'

Mike Carter and Joe ran to the front window and looked out. Pulling up their driveway was the largest car Joe had ever seen. The jet-black paintwork was polished to a high shine so that its sides gleamed like mirrors and the tall radiator and twin headlamps made it look like something that the king would drive. Joe's mouth dropped open. 'What is that car, Dad?' he breathed.

'It's a Bentley,' said his dad, sounding impressed. 'A very old one. Worth quite a bit of money if I'm not mistaken.'

The Bentley crunched to a halt on the gravel driveway and the driver's door swung open. The man who got out was older than Joe's parents,

quite short and with a large stomach that strained the buttons of his shirt. He had swept-back, white hair and a very red face and he wore a rumpled linen suit with the trousers pulled up almost to his chest.

The passenger door opened and a woman in a severe black dress got out the other side. The woman was as thin as the man was fat.

Her face was pinched and her long limbs were angular and bony so that she reminded Joe of the desk lamp in his dad's office.

'Is that them, Dad?' said Joe in a loud whisper even though they could not have heard him.

'I think so,' said his dad.

'Well, they don't look very normal to me,' said Joe.

His dad swallowed hard. 'Perhaps I'd better let them in,' he said.

They met Joe's mother coming down the stairs wearing an elegant blouse and trousers with her favourite blue sapphire necklace and matching bracelet. Her face was made up and her hair was perfect. Joe couldn't imagine how she had managed the transformation is less time than it had taken him to lay the table.

She paused at the bottom of the stairs to smooth down her clothes and take a deep breath. 'Alright,' she gasped. 'This is it, everyone.'

She took a last look in the hall mirror, then

switched on a smile as bright as a toothpaste advert before opening the front door. 'Well hell-oooooooooo there,' she gushed. 'Welcome to our humble home. We're *sooo* pleased you could make it. *Do* come in.'

The couple stood outside on the front porch with their arms linked. The man wore a tight smile, as though he had only just turned it on as the door was opened. The woman looked sour-faced and miserable, as though she had come to a funeral.

'Good *evening*, Penelope, my dear,' announced Lord Fitchwitherington in a voice that sounded like a foghorn. 'So good of you to invite us to your charming little home.'

The woman peered at Joe's mum over the top of her half-moon glasses. 'It took us quite a while to find it,' she said in an accusing voice. 'All the houses around here look exactly the same, you know.'

Lord Fitchwitherington made a show of taking

Penelope Carter's hand and kissing it, which made her cheeks turn bright pink. 'Oh, Lord Fitchwitherington,' she twittered. 'You're such a gentleman.'

'Call me Archibald, please,' he said. 'And this is my wife, Lady Fitchwitherington.'

'I suppose you can call me Margaret,' she said. 'Seeing as we're going to be neighbours soon.' She smiled in a way that made it look like she had a toothache.

'And you must be Mike,' said Lord Fitchwitherington, turning to Joe's dad. He handed him a bottle wrapped in tissue paper. 'I thought you might like to try this. We make it in the family vineyards.'

Mike Carter's eyes grew wider. 'You have your own vineyard?' he said in a hushed voice.

'Best in the country,' he said. 'You should come and visit the family estate some time. I'll give you a guided tour.'

Mike Carter beamed at the prospect of a tour

of a vineyard and Joe saw his mum and dad exchange a look to show how impressed they both were.

'And this must be young Joseph,' boomed Lord Fitchwitherington. Much to Joe's annoyance, he ruffled Joe's hair, which was one of the things he hated most in the world.

'Very pleased to make your acquaintance, young man,' he continued. 'There's someone here I'd like you to meet. This is my daughter, Miranda.'

He stepped to one side and for the first time, Joe saw that there was a young girl standing on the doorstep behind him. She was tall and very pretty, with long blonde hair tied back in a ponytail and she was dressed in a smart summer frock.

'Pleased to meet you,' she said sweetly and gave a small curtsey. 'I'm Miranda. Mother and Father have told me so much about you all.'

Joe blinked at the girl in surprise. She was taller than he remembered, and she appeared very different when she was smiling but, when he looked closer, there could be no doubt.

Miranda Fitchwitherington was the same girl who had beaten Lucy and been so rude to her that morning.

Before Joe could say anything, his mum and dad started ushering in their guests and taking their coats. Feeling bewildered, he followed them into the lounge where his dad was already deep in conversation with Lord Fitchwitherington, who was telling him about his car.

'It's a 1965 Bentley Continental,' he barked. 'She's so well soundproofed that she's as quiet as a whisper. Come and take a look. She's an absolute beauty.'

There was nothing Mike Carter liked better than talking about cars and the two men quickly headed outside to look at the Bentley, leaving Joe alone. He found his mother proudly showing off their new kitchen to Lady Fitchwitherington.

'Awfully clever how you've made the most of such a tiny space,' drawled Lady Fitchwitherington in a bored voice. 'Personally, I couldn't live without a large kitchen. I'm sure it suits you, though,' she added with a poisonous smile.

Joe tugged on his mum's sleeve. 'Mum,' he hissed. 'I need to talk to you.'

Penelope Carter gave him one of her most dangerous stares. 'Not now, Joseph,' she said through a clenched smile. 'I'm talking to our guests and guess what? I've just found out that Miranda goes to the same school as you. Isn't that wonderful?'

Joe didn't think it was wonderful at all, but he didn't get the chance to say so before his mother turned back to Miranda. 'So, how are you settling into your new school, dear?'

'It's very nice, Mrs Carter,' said Miranda politely. 'Although one of the girls I met today was really quite horrible to me.'

Joe gasped. It was Miranda who had been horrible to Lucy, not the other way around. He couldn't understand why she was now being so well-mannered and polite or why his mother seemed to be taken in by her. He grabbed a handful of peanuts from a nearby bowl and crunched them noisily to hide his annoyance.

'Oh, you poor dear,' gushed his mother. 'How awful for you. Well, it's very fortunate that you've met Joe. I'm sure he'd be delighted to show around and introduce you to his friends, wouldn't you, Joe?'

Joe nearly choked on a peanut. 'What?' he spluttered.

'Oh, that would be lovely, Mrs Carter,' said Miranda, clapping her hands together. 'That's very sweet of you, Joe.'

'Then it's settled,' said Penelope Carter in a way that made it clear that Joe had no say in the matter. 'Shall we go in for dinner?'

The two adults and Miranda moved towards the dining room and Joe watched them go, feeling very confused. If this was the same girl, then why was she now being polite and well-behaved?

Might there be two girls who looked like Miranda Fitchwitherington, one that was mean and one that was nice? He didn't have to think about it for long. At that moment, the girl looked back over her shoulder, and his blood froze.

Miranda Fitchwitherington's eyes had grown narrow and mean and her lips curled into a sneer. Then she laughed and turned away to join the adults. It had only lasted a second but there could be no mistake. She was definitely the same girl.

Dinner was awful.

For a start, octopus turned out to be the ghastliest thing Joe had ever eaten; it tasted like rubber bands boiled in vinegar. Pudding wasn't much better either. It was a sort of cold egg custard with burned sugar on top that nearly broke Joe's teeth.

All through the meal, Joe kept glancing at Miranda and, any time she thought the adults weren't looking, she would throw him back the same mean-eyed stare that made him feel cold inside.

Lord and Lady Fitchwitherington were the most boring people Joe had ever met. They talked endlessly about their houses in the country, their yacht in the Mediterranean and, worst of all, about all the important people they knew.

'Funnily enough, I said the exact same thing to the king, only a week earlier...' said Lady Fitchwitherington, finishing a story with a braying laugh.

Penelope Carter's eyes grew wide. 'You know *the king?*' she said breathlessly.

'Of course,' said Lord Fitchwitherington, as though everybody knew the king. 'Don't you?'

'Er... no,' said his dad. 'We haven't really had the opportunity...'

'Well, he comes to all of our garden parties in the summer,' he said. 'You simply must come along and meet him. Lovely man. Don't worry, he's quite used to meeting commoners.'

Penelope Carter began to glow with excitement at these words. 'The king? Really? That would be... wonderful. I must say, Archibald, we're really looking forward to having you as neighbours.'

'Oh, we're looking forward to it too, aren't we, Margaret?' said Lord Fitchwitherington, patting his wife's bony hand. 'We've always wanted a little place by the sea where we can blend in with ordinary people. In fact,' he added with a touch of pride, 'Miranda made a start this afternoon. She won the main athletics event at her new school, didn't you, dear?'

Miranda made a show of looking bashful. 'Oh, Daddy,' she said. 'It was nothing. There wasn't really very much competition.'

'Really?' Penelope Carter looked quizzically at Joe. 'I thought Lucy Yeung was running in that race, Joe? Do you mean to say she lost to Miranda?'

Joe stared at his plate and shrugged. 'I guess she was having an off day, that's all,' he said.

Penelope Carter turned to Miranda with a triumphant smile. 'Well, congratulations, my dear,' she said. 'Joe's always going on about how wonderful Lucy is at athletics. It will do him good to see there's someone better out there.' She suddenly brightened. 'I've got a good idea. Why doesn't Joe spend some time tomorrow showing Miranda around Southwold. Joe would like that, wouldn't you, Joe?'

Joe swallowed. 'Er, I dunno,' he mumbled. 'I was going to the beach hut to meet the others.'

'Beach hut?' Lord Fitchwitherington was suddenly interested. 'I say, Carter,' he said to Joe's dad. 'You never told me you had a beach hut. I've been meaning to buy one of those for Miranda, but you can't buy them for love nor money.'

Penelope Carter turned on her brightest estate agent's smile. 'Archibald, I didn't know you wanted a beach hut. Perhaps you should take a look at ours. We've never really used it and, to be honest, it's just going to waste.'

Poor Joe could not believe what he was hearing. 'It's not going to waste,' he cried. 'It's our clubhouse.'

'Well, if you're serious about selling,' said Lord Fitchwitherington, 'I'd make you a very fair offer. Miranda's got her heart set on having one, haven't you, dear?'

Mike Carter glanced at his wife, who gave him an enthusiastic nod. 'I suppose we *might* consider it,' he said slowly. 'If the price was right, of course.'

'*Dad!*' exclaimed Joe. 'You... you can't sell the beach hut. You said we could use it. Tell her she can't have it—'

'That's *enough*, Joseph,' said his mother sharply. 'We let you use it to play detectives with your friends, but it was only a temporary arrangement. If Lord Fitchwitherington wants to buy it then you'll just have to find somewhere else.'

Joe opened his mouth to object but his mother gave him a glare that could have frozen water.

'Excellent news, Carter,' Lord Fitchwitherington was saying. 'When could we take a look at the place?'

'How about tomorrow?' said Joe's mum quickly.

Lord Fitchwitherington frowned. 'Margaret and I are busy tomorrow,' he said. 'We have to go back to London for an event at the House of Lords. It's an awful bore, but Miranda could go, couldn't you, dear? I trust her judgement completely.'

'Of course I can,' said Miranda. She looked at Joe with a nasty gleam in her eye. 'Perhaps Joe could take me?'

'Fantastic idea,' said Penelope. 'Joe would be delighted, wouldn't you, dear? And you can introduce Miranda to all your little friends. I'm sure you're all going to get on really well.'

5

THE AWFUL MIRANDA FITCHWITHERINGTON

Lucy gritted her teeth and felt the burn in her stomach muscles as she struggled to sit up with her hands clasped behind her head.

'How many is that?' she gasped as she paused to take a breath.

On the other side of the beach hut, Max looked up from his book and blinked at her owlishly from behind his glasses. 'What? Oh, er... probably about fifty.'

Lucy frowned. 'You said that five minutes ago. You said you'd count my sit-ups for me but all you've done is sit there with your nose buried in that stupid book.'

Max looked hurt. *'The Adventures of Sherlock Holmes* is not just "some stupid book",' he said. 'Holmes was a genius detective who was brilliant at finding clues that other people missed. I was reading this because I thought Holmes could help us find the dognappers.'

'How's he going to do that?' said Lucy.

'Well, in one of the stories, Holmes used a trained bloodhound to follow the scent of the criminals and track them back to their hideout. Perhaps we could do that?'

Lucy scratched her head. 'We don't know anyone with a bloodhound,' she said. 'And, even if we did, I don't think they're going to lend us their dog to track down the dognappers. Now, are you going to count my sit-ups or not?'

Max sighed and closed his book. 'I don't understand why anyone needs to sit up that many times,' he said. 'I'm sure I could design a mechanical chair that would take all of the hard work out of it for you.'

'The hard work is the whole point,' said Lucy. 'After I lost the race yesterday, I promised my dad I'd step up my training. He said every top athlete learns from their defeats and it makes them stronger.'

Max laughed. 'Well, you know my motto, Luce,' he said. *'If at first you don't succeed, it's too difficult.* Why don't we call it an even seventy-five and have a cup of tea instead?'

Lucy sighed and got up to put on the kettle, reminding herself not to ask Max for help with her training in future. She was dropping the tea bags into the pot when the door burst open and Charlie pushed her way inside, dragging Sherlock after her.

As soon as he was inside, Sherlock flopped down on the rug and rested his head on his paws with a very forlorn expression. 'What's up with Sherlock?' said Lucy. 'He's usually looking for a biscuit by now.'

'He's sulking, because I won't let him off the lead,' said Charlie. 'All the way here he was trying to get away to chase the seagulls.'

At the mention of the word 'seagulls', Sherlock sighed and his head sank deeper between his paws. All the way along the promenade, he had eyed the fat, lazy seagulls gathered on the beach. He was absolutely sure he could have caught one if only Charlie had let him go.

'Well, why is he on the lead?' said Max. 'I've never seen you use it before.'

'Because of the dognappers, of course,' said Charlie. 'I'd never forgive myself if a dognapper took Sherlock.'

'I'm sure you don't need to worry too much,'

said Lucy kindly. 'My dad said that after the gang have been in the area for a few days, they'll go somewhere else where people are less on their guard.'

'But they *are* still here,' insisted Charlie. 'Haven't you heard? Another dog was stolen this morning.'

'*Another* one?' said Max. 'Who from?'

'From Mr Pickering, at the amusement arcade,' said Charlie. 'He left his Labrador, Morrie, in his back garden while he was making dinner. When he went out again half an hour later, Morrie was gone.'

'That's terrible,' said Lucy.

'And it means that the dognappers are still in Southwold,' said Max.

'That's what I'm trying to tell you,' said Charlie. 'And that's why I can't let Sherlock out of my sight. It's too dangerous.'

'I don't understand how they can take all these dogs without being seen,' said Lucy. 'Surely somebody noticed something?'

'We should do some investigating of our own,' said Max. 'We could try Sherlock Holmes's methods. Sometimes he'd catch criminals by setting a trap.'

'A trap?' said Lucy. 'What sort of trap?'

Max thought for a moment. 'Well, what if we tied Sherlock up to a lamp post and then hid behind a bush. Then if anyone came along and tried to take him—'

'No way!' Charlie slammed her fist down on the table with such ferocity that Max almost fell off the seat. 'You are not going to use my dog as bait, Max Green. I'm not allowing him anywhere near those dognappers.' She pulled Sherlock closer and glared angrily at Max, who had the decency to look ashamed.

'I'm sorry,' he said. 'It was just an idea.'

'One of your worst,' said Charlie with a scowl.

'I'm sure Max didn't mean anything by it,' said Lucy. 'But perhaps he's right. Maybe we could do a bit of detective work to see if we can spot anything suspicious.'

The door swung open again and Joe walked in with drooped shoulders and a look of gloom on his face.

'What's up with you?' said Max. 'You look like I did when I dropped my phone down the toilet.'

Joe looked around glumly. 'Sorry I'm late,' he said in a dull voice. 'But I've brought someone with me. This is Miranda Fitchwitherington.'

For the first time, they saw the girl standing behind him. She brushed past Joe and looked around the little beach hut with a sneer on her lips. 'So, this is the famous beach hut, is it?' she said. 'I must say, it's a bit pokier in here than I imagined. And I guess this is the so-called After-School Detective Club?'

Sherlock gave a low growl and the others stared, open-mouthed. It was Lucy who spoke first. 'What are *you* doing here?' she said crossly.

Miranda looked down her nose at Lucy as though she was noticing her for the first time. 'Oh, look, it's the loser,' she said. 'Lost any good races lately?'

Lucy clenched her fists and glared angrily at the girl. 'I'll have you know I've won plenty of races.'

Miranda gave a silvery laugh. 'It's easy to win races when you haven't got any competition,' she said. 'But now I'm here, and you know what they say.' She gave a small flick of her ponytail. 'Once a loser, always a loser.'

'You've got no right to talk to Lucy that way,'

said Max, standing next to his friend. 'Lucy's a really good athlete.'

Miranda looked down at Max and raised an eyebrow. 'And what would *you* know about being an athlete,' she said. 'You look like you've never run anywhere in your life.' Before Max could stop her, Miranda reached out and prodded him in the belly with her forefinger.

Max gasped and took a step backwards, covering his belly with his arms. 'Don't...' he gasped. 'D-don't do that. You've got no right...' He swallowed hard and his lower lip trembled, to Miranda's obvious delight.

Lucy stepped in front of Max and faced Miranda angrily. Her cheeks flushed red. 'You leave him alone!' she cried. 'You've got no right to talk to him like that.'

Miranda's eyes opened wide in mock-surprise. 'Oh, look at that, geek boy,' she said. 'Your girlfriend's come to rescue you.'

Sherlock had been watching closely and had

decided that he did not like this new girl. He had growled when she prodded Max, but now she was being horrible to Lucy as well, it was too much for a little dog to bear. With a loud bark, he leaped forwards with his teeth bared. Miranda stepped back in alarm and Sherlock jerked to a halt as Charlie pulled him back on the lead.

For a brief moment, there was a look of fear in Miranda's eyes but she quickly regained her composure when she realised Sherlock couldn't reach her. 'What a scruffy little mongrel.' She sniffed. Then she looked Charlie up and down disapprovingly. 'Mind you, I can see why he's so scruffy if *you're* his owner. They say dogs and their owners grow to look alike.'

Charlie's face turned white with rage. 'Sherlock is *not* a mongrel,' she insisted. She looked like she was ready to bite the girl herself, but Lucy placed a restraining hand on Charlie's arm.

'Joe, this girl's being horrible to everyone,' said Lucy. 'Why have you brought her here?'

Poor Joe looked as miserable and ashamed as they had ever seen him. He stared down at his feet and shrugged his shoulders. 'I'm really sorry,' he mumbled. 'I didn't have any choice. Her dad's an important client of my mum's. I *had* to bring her.'

'But why here, Joe?' said Max miserably. 'The beach hut is *our* meeting place. If she can't behave properly then she's got no right being here.'

Miranda gave a nasty laugh. 'That's where you're wrong,' she said. 'I have *every* right to be here. Daddy has asked me to come and look at your precious beach hut because he wants to buy it for me. And if I tell him that I want it, then it won't be yours for much longer.'

Max, Lucy and Charlie reeled in shock at this new information. They looked at Joe, and the expression on his face told them that it was true.

It was Max who spoke first. 'And *do* you want it?' he said in a small voice.

Miranda shrugged and made an undecided

face. 'It's a bit tatty in here,' she said, looking at the yellowing newspaper clippings about the After-School Detective Club that Max had stuck to the wall. 'It could do with repainting. I'm thinking, maybe, bright pink.'

'Bright pink!' they all chorused.

'And these sofas are disgusting,' continued Miranda. She felt one of the cushions and made a face, then wiped her fingers on her trousers. 'Everything's covered in dog hair; they'll all have to go. Besides, I'll need to make room for my speakers.'

'Speakers?' said Charlie.

'Great big ones,' said Miranda with a smile. 'You can't have a good time at the beach without some really loud music.'

'You can't do that,' said Lucy. 'You'll disturb all the other people who want to use the beach.'

Miranda waved a dismissive hand. 'Who cares about other people,' she said. 'If they don't like it, they can just go somewhere else.' She took a last look around the room. 'Yes, it will need a lot of work, but I think it will suit me very well. I'm going to tell Daddy to buy it for me.'

'Y-you can't.'

Everybody turned to look at Joe. While Miranda had been speaking, he had become more and more miserable until he could stand it no longer. 'This place belongs to us,' he said defiantly. 'This is our clubhouse and you can't have it. Once I tell my parents what a horrible person you really are, they won't sell it to your dad. You'll see.'

Miranda threw back her head and laughed. 'That's the funniest thing I've ever heard,' she gasped. 'Well, I've got news for you, Joe Carter,' she said. 'Your parents will sell this place to us because Daddy is a rich and important client and they have to do what he wants. People with money always get what they want – you'll learn.'

She turned to leave, then paused in the doorway. 'I want to get started on the decorating as soon as possible, so if you could have your stuff out of here by the end of the week, that would be great.'

'The end of the week?' said Max weakly.

'And I'll need your key, too, Joe,' she said. 'Tell your parents that Daddy will drop by to pick it up this evening.' She gave them all a nasty smile. 'Well, goodbye, *After-School Detective Club,*' she said. 'It's been nice doing business with you.'

6

MORE BAD NEWS

Nobody spoke for a long while after Miranda Fitchwitherington had left. They had met people who were rude or unpleasant before, but they had never come across anyone as downright nasty as Miranda.

'She is the most *horrible* person I've ever met,' spluttered Lucy eventually.

'She managed to be rude to all of us in less than ten minutes,' said Max.

'Sherlock hated her on sight,' said Charlie. 'And he's never wrong.'

Joe slumped down on the sofa and put his head in his hands. 'I'm sorry,' he said miserably.

'I didn't want to bring her here, but I didn't have any choice.'

'Isn't there any way you can stop your parents from selling the beach hut to her dad?' said Max.

Joe shook his head sadly. 'I don't see how,' he said. 'My mum thinks Lord Fitchwitherington is going to buy an expensive house. She'll insist my dad sells him this place to keep him happy.'

Max shrugged dismally. 'Well, I guess we'll have to find somewhere else to meet,' he said. 'I don't know anywhere that would be as good as this place, though,' he added.

Charlie picked one of the newspaper clippings off the wall and looked at it sadly. 'It won't be the same if we can't come here,' she said. 'It will be like we're not the After-School Detective Club any more.'

Lucy blew out a big sigh. 'This is no good,' she said. 'We can't spend the whole day moping around here. Let's walk down to the harbour to cheer ourselves up.'

Nobody felt much like being cheerful, but they all agreed that there wasn't much point in sitting around in the beach hut. Besides, it didn't feel quite the same now that they knew Miranda was making plans to move in and paint it bright pink.

They headed outside and Joe locked the door before they set out towards the harbour. 'Do you really think Miranda will move into the beach hut this weekend?' said Max as they walked.

'I expect so,' said Joe. 'My mum will do anything to make sure Lord Fitchwitherington gets what he wants.'

'Look,' said Charlie, pointing. 'There's that dreadful girl again.' On the far side of the road, they saw Miranda talking to the driver of an enormous black car parked there.

'That's the Fitchwitheringtons' Bentley,' said Joe. 'That's strange. Lord Fitchwitherington said that he and his wife had to be in London today.'

'Miranda's probably telling them what fools she made of us,' said Max. 'I think I hate her more

than anyone I've ever met.' Sherlock growled in agreement and pulled on his lead.

Miranda opened the car door and climbed inside and then the powerful Bentley glided away along the seafront. 'Good riddance,' said Lucy firmly. 'If I never see her again it will be too soon.'

It was a pleasant walk to the harbour in the sunshine, though none of them were really in the mood to enjoy it. Several people were out walking their dogs, although nearly all of them were being kept firmly on the lead, just like Sherlock. They had not gone much further when they saw a familiar figure coming towards them, wearing his sailor's pea jacket and a nautical cap.

'It's Captain Tom,' said Lucy happily. 'And he's got Pugly with him.'

When Sherlock saw Pugly, he cheered up immediately. The two dogs strained at their leads to get to each other and then spent several minutes sniffing various parts of each other in greeting. But if Pugly and Sherlock were pleased to see each other, the expression on the captain's leathery face was decidedly anxious. He held Pugly on a very short leash and kept glancing over his shoulder as though he thought someone might be following him.

'What's wrong, Captain Tom?' said Charlie. 'You look really worried.'

'Ain't you 'eard?' he said in a hushed voice. 'There's been another dognapping.'

'Another one?' gasped Charlie. She instinctively pulled Sherlock closer. 'Where?'

'From Mrs Bannerjee up on North Road,' said Tom. 'She tied her two pedigree poodles up outside the newsagent's. She was only in there for a minute, but when she came out, they were gone.'

'Did anyone see who did it?' said Max.

'No one saw a thing,' said Tom. 'It was as if the ground had opened up and swallowed them dogs whole. Poor Mrs Bannerjee loves those dogs as if they were her own children.' He shook his head sadly. 'I'm getting too worried to even take Pugly out of doors. We only came out for a quick walk around the block and now I'm taking him straight home. You young folks take care now.'

Captain Tom hurried away down the road, keeping Pugly close to his heels. Charlie had turned quite pale when she heard Tom's story. Now she bent down and scooped up Sherlock into her arms as though he might disappear right before her eyes. 'I think I should take Sherlock home,' she said.

Lucy placed a reassuring hand on Charlie's arm. 'Don't worry,' she said. 'He'll be safe while we're all together.'

'Yes,' said Joe. 'If anyone tries to steal him, they'll have to deal with us first.'

'I'm sure it will be alright, Charlie,' said Max.

But Charlie could not be consoled. She blinked rapidly and there were tears in her eyes. 'No, it's not going to be alright,' she blurted. Too many dogs have gone missing already and I'm not going to let them steal Sherlock too. I'm sorry but I'm going to have to take him home right now.'

Before anyone could argue, she turned in the direction of home and walked away quickly, clutching Sherlock in her arms.

'Poor Charlie,' said Joe. 'She really is very worried about him.'

'Poor Sherlock,' said Max. 'I don't think he's ever going to be allowed to walk anywhere ever again.'

Lucy hugged herself as though she was feeling cold. 'This has been such a horrible day,' she said. 'First, we get thrown out of the beach hut, and now more dogs are missing. Something very strange is happening in Southwold.'

They all agreed miserably that things did not feel at all as they should. Joe glanced at his watch. 'I really ought to go too,' he said. 'Mum has to work late and she asked me to prepare the vegetables for tea. I'd better try and stay in her good books if I'm going to stand any chance of persuading my parents to keep the beach hut.'

'Do you think they will?' said Max hopefully.

Joe shook his head. 'I don't think so,' he said. 'Once my mum's mind is made up about something, it usually stays that way.' He raised a hand in farewell and started off in the direction of his own house.

'So, it's just you and me then, Luce,' said Max, after Joe had left. 'Shall we go and get an ice cream?'

Lucy shook her head. 'Can't do it, I'm afraid,' she said. 'I promised Dad I'd do another training run this afternoon. I'd better go too. See you.'

Max watched his friend jog away towards her house and then he let out a sigh. It was true, he thought, things really didn't feel right in Southwold at the moment. Losing the beach hut was bad enough, but it was awful that people didn't feel safe to walk their own dogs. If only there was something the After-School Detective Club could do about it.

He glanced down at the book in his hand. *If only we had a bloodhound like Sherlock Holmes, we might be able to track down the dognappers*, he thought. But Max was not even sure what a bloodhound looked like, let alone know anyone who owned one.

Then, as it often did when Max was thinking about a particularly difficult problem, an idea came to him in a flash. Perhaps, there was something he could do after all. He might not be able to get hold of a real bloodhound but he could do the next best thing.

He could make one.

Then he smiled to himself. What he had in mind would be difficult to do, but, if he succeeded, it could be the After-School Detective Club's greatest triumph. He walked slowly towards his house, deep in thought as he ran through a list of the things he would need.

Max was so preoccupied that he failed to notice the strange black van that cruised past him along the main promenade. He didn't see the driver, or the darkened windows and he certainly didn't hear the sounds of muffled barking that came from inside.

Only as it turned into one of the side streets did Max look up from his book and catch a glimpse of the van disappearing around the corner. He stared after it for a few moments, then shrugged and continued walking.

7

GROUP CHAT

Charlie: Hlo? Is nyone els up yt?

Joe: Hey, Charlie. It's really early. Is everything OK?

Charlie: Ys – jst a bt bord – % me n S.Lock hvnt bn out snce Sundy

Joe: I can hardly understand what you're typing. I can't believe you still use that old phone

Charlie: Im kpng it jst 2 anoy U

Joe: Did you say you haven't been out since Sunday? That's no way to spend half-term.

Charlie: I kno – bt im 2 worrid 2 tk hm out in cse he gts dgnpped %** Wht hv u bn doing?

Joe: Trying to stay out of the way of the Fitchwitheringtons. Mum's been with them all week – she says they've seen nearly every house for sale in Southwold.

Charlie: Hvnt thy bght nythng yt?

Joe: No but Mum's convinced they will soon and that she'll be made 'employee of the month'. The worst thing is, every time she shows them a house she insists on bringing them back to our house for a 'debrief'.

Charlie: Wht? Evn Mirnda?

Joe: Oh yeah, especially Miranda. The worst thing is that Miranda is always so polite and nice when she's here that Mum thinks she's wonderful. She keeps trying to get me to hang out with her – she says Miranda 'would be a better class of friend' for me.

Charlie: Ugh!

Lucy: Hey guys, what's new?

Joe: Charlie and Sherlock are never leaving the house again.

Charlie: Thts nt tru! %% Im jst bng crful thts al *

Lucy: I don't think you need to worry too much.

My dad said there haven't been any more dognappings since the weekend. Maybe they've moved on to somewhere else.

Charlie: Hs nyone hrd frm MaX?% Hes bn vrY quet ltly.

Lucy: I asked him if he wanted to come to the library yesterday, but he said he was too busy.

Charlie: He ddnt wnt 2 go 2 the lbry? He mst be sck!

Joe: He's not sick. I went round to see him last night. He's working on a top-secret project to catch the dognappers but I'm not allowed to tell you about it.

Lucy: Why on earth not?

Joe: He says he wants to keep it a surprise. It's absolutely brilliant but he made me swear not to tell you.

Charlie: If he trstd u wth a scret thn he's mre stupd thn I tht.

Max: Hey, guys! What's happening?

Joe: Max. We were just talking about you.

Max: Brilliant. I love it when people talk about me. It's even better than when I talk about me.

Charlie: Was ur hed alwys ths bg or did it jst gro fster thn th rst of ur body? *

Lucy: Joe says you've been working on a secret project but he won't tell us what it is.

Max: You bet I have. Sherlock Holmes would be proud of me. It's one of my most genius ideas yet.

Lucy: It's not like the time you tried to convert your house to solar energy and blew all the street lamps in your road, is it?

Max: That was just a small miscalculation on my part.

Joe: Yeah, you miscalculated the bit about your mum grounding you for a week.

Max: This is completely different. It's going to keep Sherlock safe and it's going to help us catch the dognappers.

Lucy: Well, tells us what it is! Joe won't tell us anything.

Max: That's because I wanted to show you in person. Can we all get together?

Joe: Good idea. Let's meet at the beach hut.

Max: Really? I thought your dad made you return the key when he agreed to sell the beach hut to Lord F?

Joe: He did, but I know where he keeps the spare key. We can use that one.

Lucy: I'm not sure that's a good idea, Joe.

Joe: Well, why not? The beach hut still belongs to us until the sale goes through. There's no reason why we shouldn't use it.

Charlie: Wll im in fvor of nythng that hlps 2 kp S.LoCk sfe. Lts do it!

Max: Excellent! I'll see you all there in an hour. It's about time we gave those dognappers a taste of the After-School Detective Club!

8

AN UNWELCOME VISITOR

Joe was in such a hurry to get to the beach hut for Max's big surprise that he wasn't watching where he was going. As he crossed the road, a horn blared suddenly and he leaped back onto the pavement just in time as a speeding vehicle flashed past him.

Joe looked at the black van as it disappeared up the road and wondered where he had seen it before. He was still thinking when he heard a shout behind him.

'Hey, Joe, wait up. It's us!'

He turned to see Charlie and Sherlock sprinting

up the road behind him. Charlie looked nervous and pale and kept glancing over her shoulder. She still had Sherlock on the lead but at least he looked happy to be outdoors.

'Hey, guys, great to see you,' said Joe. He crouched down to make a fuss of Sherlock and then they walked on together.

'So, are you going to tell me what Max's secret project is?' said Charlie.

'Wild horses wouldn't drag it out of me,' said Joe importantly. 'He made me promise not to tell anyone. Besides, here's Max and Lucy now. You can ask him yourself.'

Max and Lucy were hurrying towards them from the other direction. Max was carrying his backpack and looking very pleased with himself. When they met, there was a pause while Sherlock greeted them with slobbery licks until Charlie could contain herself no longer.

'Alright,' she said. 'That's enough licking, Sherlock. If Max won't tell me his secret right now,

I think I'm going to burst.'

'It's no use,' said Lucy. 'I've been trying to get him to tell me all the way here. I can't stand the idea that Joe knows and we don't.'

Max adopted a very superior face. 'This is not the place to discuss it, Luce,' he said in a snooty voice. He glanced over his shoulder and then dropped his voice to a stage whisper. 'There might be spies on every street corner.'

'I think you're enjoying this a bit too much,' said Lucy with a frown.

'You can't be too careful with dognappers around,' said Max with a sniff. 'Come on, let's get to the beach hut and have a cup of tea, then I'll tell you everything.'

They continued along the promenade, but, as they drew closer to the hut, something did not look right. Joe was the first to notice.

'The door's open,' he gasped. 'And I know I locked it last time.'

They approached slowly, hearing the sounds

of banging from inside and tinny music being played on speakers that were too small. When they looked through the doorway, they saw at once the reason for the noise. Sherlock growled and Charlie had to tighten her grip on his leash.

In the centre of the beach hut, Miranda Fitchwitherington was surrounded by cardboard boxes, into which she had piled cushions, towels, mugs, plates, saucepans and rugs. She had even removed Max's newspaper clippings from the wall and stuffed them into one of the overloaded boxes.

'What are you doing in here?' cried Joe. 'You've got no right to—'

'Actually, I've got every right,' snapped Miranda. 'Your dad signed the papers this morning and my father wrote him a cheque. By the end of the week, this place will belong to me and there's nothing you can do about it.' She looked around at the boxes and wrinkled her nose in disgust. 'You should be grateful that I've cleared out all

your mess for you. I don't know what your parents were thinking, letting you use this place to play at detectives.'

Max pulled one of the newspaper clippings out of the nearest box and looked at it sadly. It had been torn nearly in half when Miranda had ripped it off the wall. 'We weren't playing at being detectives,' he said quietly. 'We *are* detectives.'

'Don't make me laugh,' said Miranda. 'You lot couldn't solve a crime if it happened right under your noses.'

'We can too,' said Lucy. 'We've solved lots of crimes.'

'Yeah?' said Miranda in a mocking tone. 'Well, what about all the dognappings in Southwold, then? You haven't solved those, have you?'

'Maybe not yet,' said Joe. 'But we're going to. Max has got a plan to catch them, haven't you, Max?'

Miranda raised an interested eyebrow. 'Have you, Max?' she said. 'Well, that's very interesting.

I've read all the newspaper reports about "Max Green, the child genius". So come on then, what's your great plan?' She folded her arms and looked at Max with a mocking smile.

Max frowned at Joe. 'That was meant to be a secret,' he hissed.

Miranda threw back her head and laughed. 'You seriously expect me to believe you've got a secret plan?' she said. 'You're nothing but a big loser, just like your friend. In fact, you should all be called the After-School *Losers* Club.' She looked thoughtful for a moment. 'Maybe I could make that into a thing?'

Max, Lucy and Charlie scowled and Sherlock had to be held firmly on his lead. But no one was as angry as Joe.

It was bad enough that Miranda was going to take their precious beach hut. And it was hugely frustrating that his mum thought Miranda was so wonderful when she was so horrible. But the worst thing of all was hearing Miranda making fun of the After-School Detective Club. Joe wanted to say something, anything, that would show her that they were proper detectives.

'We have got a plan to catch the dognappers,' he blurted suddenly.

'Joe...' warned Max.

'Max has built a special device that can be attached to a dog's collar so we can find them if they get stolen,' he said.

As soon as it was out, Joe realised he shouldn't have said it. Max's expression was furious. 'Joe!' he spluttered. 'You weren't supposed to tell anyone, least of all *her!*'

Miranda looked on with amusement, and then doubled up with laughter. She laughed so long and so hard that real tears began to run down her face and she fought to catch her breath. 'Is... is that *it?*' she gasped when she could finally talk. 'Is that your great plan to catch the dognappers? A *tracking device?* That won't work in a million years.'

'It *is* going to work!' said Max, furious at being laughed at. 'I built it myself and I know it will.'

'Well, I think it's a genius idea, Max,' said Charlie. 'And who cares what *she* thinks.'

'I agree,' said Lucy. 'I think it's really sweet of you, Max. I'm sure every dog owner around here will want one.'

Miranda was now dabbing at her eyes with a tissue. 'No dognapper is going to be fooled by that,' she said. 'You kids are really stupid.'

'Alright, that's enough,' shouted Joe. 'I don't care if your dad is an important client. It doesn't give you the right to be rude to my friends. And this beach hut doesn't belong to you until the weekend, so you can get out and don't come back until then.'

For a moment, Miranda looked ready to argue. But Joe's clenched fists and red face made her think twice. She looked around the angry faces and then shrugged her shoulders.

'I don't care,' she said. 'You can keep your stupid

beach hut for now. Just make sure you have all your junk out of here by the weekend or I'll have it sent to the dump.' She picked up the tinny speaker that was still blaring in the corner of the room, then shoved rudely past them.

9

THE ELECTRONIC NOSE

After Miranda Fitchwitherington had left, slamming the door behind her, everyone was silent for a long time. It was Joe who spoke first.

'I'm sorry, Max,' he blurted. 'I didn't mean to tell her about your plan, but she was being so horrible that I just wanted to show her she was wrong.' He slumped onto the bare sofa and held his head in his hands. 'I wanted her to know that you do invent cool stuff and that we really have caught lots of criminals.'

Max dropped down on the sofa next to Joe. 'It's alright,' he said. 'I think Miranda Fitchwitherington has a way of getting under everyone's skin.'

'Why would anyone want to be like that?' said Joe. He looked around at the boxes, packed with the things that had made the beach hut feel like such a special place, and he began to feel sad all over again.

'I think she actually enjoys upsetting other people,' said Lucy. 'The more we get angry with her, the more she likes it. We have to do our best to try and ignore her.'

'Let's talk about something else for a change,' said Charlie. She had finally let Sherlock off his lead and the little dog was so excited that he promptly bounded all over the furniture, licking faces and getting even more muddy pawprints on the sofa. 'Why don't you show us your invention, Max? It sounds really interesting.'

Max grinned. 'Yeah, I am pretty proud of it,' he said. 'But before I show you, how about we put the beach hut back the way it was, even if we only have it for a few more days. It doesn't feel right without all our stuff in it.'

They agreed this was an excellent idea and spent the next fifteen minutes unpacking rugs, cushions, mugs and the teapot from Miranda's boxes. Then Joe put on the kettle while Charlie gave Sherlock some dry dog food and Lucy helped Max lift the table back in front of the sofa.

When they were all seated with a mug of hot tea and a packet of custard creams, Max began. 'So, I was reading Sherlock Holmes...' he said.

Everyone groaned. 'Not Sherlock Holmes *again*,' said Charlie. 'I don't see how a hundred-year-old detective is going to help us catch the dognappers.'

'That's where you're wrong,' said Max triumphantly. 'Do you remember I told you that Sherlock Holmes used a bloodhound to follow the criminal's scent? Well, I have invented an electronic bloodhound.'

'An electronic bloodhound?' said Lucy, starting to giggle. 'It must have a very long lead.'

'How do you switch it off?' said Charlie. 'Does it have a paws button?'

'If it works by remote control, perhaps it's a golden receiver,' added Joe.

The three of them doubled up with laughter, slapping each other on the back and rolling about on the sofa until Max became quite cross.

'Cut it out, you lot,' he snapped. 'This is serious science I'm talking about.'

'Sorry, Max,' said Lucy wiping her eyes. 'You haven't really built a whole robot dog, have you?'

'I don't have to,' said Max. 'Bloodhounds use their noses to track people by following a scent trail. I've built an artificial "nose" that can follow an electronic trail in the same way.' He reached into his bag and pulled out a mobile phone, attached to a hefty battery with several wrappings of insulating tape. There was also a long, bendy aerial with a small red light at the end of it. 'Behold!' he said. 'The electronic nose.'

The others peered at the device curiously. 'What does it do?' said Joe.

'It picks up a trail of electro-magnetic impulses,

and projects them onto a map, here.' Max pointed to the phone's screen. 'If a dog gets stolen, I can use this device to track it down in minutes.'

'I don't know what electro-magnetic impulses are,' said Charlie, 'but I'm pretty sure that dogs don't leave a trail of them.'

'Aha,' said Max, reaching into his bag again. 'They do if they're wearing one of these.'

He took out a narrow strip of brown leather with a small buckle on it and laid it on the table next to the 'electronic nose'. The others looked at it curiously. 'It's just a dog collar,' said Charlie.

'It *looks* like a dog collar,' said Max. 'But it contains some highly sophisticated circuitry, cunningly hidden inside the collar. It was really hard to make it that small – that's why it took me so long – but if a dog gets stolen while they're wearing one of these, we can track them wherever they are.'

The gang examined the collar and even Sherlock gave it a sniff. 'It's tiny,' said Charlie. 'Can you really track a missing dog using that?'

'Sure can,' said Max. 'Watch this. Excuse me, Sherlock.'

He gave Sherlock a pat on the head and then reached the collar around his neck and fastened it. 'Will it bother him?' said Lucy.

'I don't think so,' said Max. 'I made it as light as possible so he wouldn't know he was wearing it.'

Sherlock wagged his tail vigorously as though to demonstrate how much it wasn't bothering him. He couldn't quite understand why the children were so interested in him all of a sudden, but he was quite enjoying the attention.

'And can you really track him wherever he goes now?' said Joe.

'Simple,' said Max, looking very pleased with himself. 'Watch this.' He tapped a few keys and the electronic nose suddenly bloomed to life in a flurry of lights and bleeping noises. A map of Southwold appeared on the tiny screen with, a pulsing blue dot right in the centre.

'See that,' said Max. 'That's Sherlock, right there.

Now we'll always know where he is.'

'Oh Max, that's brilliant,' gasped Charlie. She had been very quiet while Max was demonstrating the collar. She had been concerned that Sherlock would find it uncomfortable or that it wouldn't work properly. But as soon as she saw it working, she broke out in a huge smile. 'I'm still going to worry about him,' she said. 'But at least I know I'll be able to find him again if he gets lost.'

Without warning, she threw her arms around Max and gave him a big hug. Max looked startled but also quite pleased and Sherlock barked excitedly so that they all broke out in smiles and the awful Miranda Fitchwitherington was forgotten. Because, however terrible things may seem, they can always be made better when you're with your friends.

'So, what about the other dogs in Southwold?' said Joe. 'Have you got a collar for all of them?'

Max shook his head. 'Not yet,' he said. 'I only had time to make two; this one is for Sherlock and I've got another one in my bag for Pugly. I'm going to give it to Captain Tom when I see him. But now that I know how to make them, it will be a lot quicker to build the next ones.'

'Well, I think it's brilliant,' said Charlie. 'And Sherlock seems happy enough.'

Sherlock did not seem particularly interested in his new collar and had settled down on the rug for a doze. Sherlock regarded collars as just one of those strange things that humans did, like making their dogs wear coats or bows in their hair.

At least they had not made him do that.

'The trouble is, it only solves half the problem,' said Lucy.

Max frowned. 'What do you mean?'

'Well, ideally, we want to find out who's behind this *before* they steal someone's dog,' said Lucy.

'Maybe we could ask an eyewitness,' said Joe helpfully. 'That's what the police do on the TV when there's been a murder.'

'There hasn't been a murder,' said Charlie, with a frown. 'And there aren't any eyewitnesses either. From what I hear, everyone who's lost their dog said they didn't see or hear anything. That's what I don't understand; if someone tried to steal Sherlock, he'd bark his head off.'

'Perhaps they're putting the dogs into something so that no one can hear them barking,' said Joe. 'Like a van with soundproofing on the inside.'

Charlie scratched her head. 'It's possible, I suppose,' she said. 'But I don't think we've seen anything like that around here.'

'Wait a minute,' said Lucy. 'We *have* seen something like that. The other evening, just before we met Captain Tom, we saw a black van, speeding down the street.'

Max gasped. 'I saw it a second time,' he said. 'When I was on my way home. It drove right past me.'

Joe snapped his fingers. 'And I saw it today,' he said. 'When I was on my way here, I nearly stepped in front of it. It had dark windows and everything. Do you really think it could be the van the dognappers are using?'

'It must be,' said Lucy. 'Did you ever see it before the dognappings started?' They all shook their heads. 'Well, there you are,' she said. 'Southwold is a small place. If it belonged to someone we knew, we'd have been bound to notice it before now. It must belong to the dognappers.'

'Joe, did you say you saw it on the way here?' said Max. Joe nodded. 'Well, that means it's in town right now. It's probably out looking for more dogs while we speak.'

'You're right,' said Charlie. 'We should call the police straight away.'

'Why would they believe us?' said Joe. 'We haven't got any evidence; it's just a theory.'

'We should try and find the van first,' said Max. 'Who knows, we might even catch them in the act.'

'How are we going to find it?' said Lucy.

'It can't be far away,' said Max. 'If we search all the side streets, we should find it in no time.'

'And then what?' said Lucy. 'It's not like we can arrest the dognappers ourselves, is it?'

'Then we just keep an eye on the van and wait for the police to arrive,' said Max. 'The dognappers won't even know we're there. It'll be perfectly safe.'

Joe clapped his hands together. 'Brilliant idea, Max,' he said. 'It will be like being on a proper stakeout, waiting for the criminals to turn up like they do on TV.'

'You haven't said much, Charlie,' said Lucy. 'What do you think?'

While the others were discussing the plan, Charlie had been quiet and thoughtful. 'I'm not sure,' she said slowly. 'I mean, I'd like to catch the dognappers but I don't want to take Sherlock anywhere near them. I should take him home first, so that I know he's safe.'

'We don't have time for that,' said Max. 'If we wait for you to go home and come back again, the dognappers could get away.'

Charlie scowled. 'I don't care,' she snapped. 'I'm not taking my dog anywhere near that van.'

'What if we left him here?' said Joe. 'I've still got the key, so we can lock him inside. He'll be perfectly safe.' He held up the spare key he had taken from his father's bedside table.

Charlie looked unconvinced. 'I-I'm not sure,' she said. 'I don't think Sherlock would like it being locked in a strange place on his own.'

'It's hardly a strange place,' said Joe. 'Sherlock

comes here all the time. We can leave him some dry food and he'll go to sleep like he always does. Trust me, Charlie, he'll be fine.'

Charlie bit her lip. She was worried about Sherlock but she also wanted to go hunting for the dognappers. She looked down at the little dog, who had indeed curled up on the rug and gone to sleep the way he always did. She had to admit that he would probably be perfectly happy left where he was.

'Alright,' she said eventually. 'We'll leave him here. But you have to make sure you lock that door properly, Joe. I'm trusting you.'

'I promise,' said Joe at once. 'He'll be completely safe, you'll see.'

'I'll take the electronic nose with me,' said Max. 'That way we can check up on Sherlock while we're out.' He took the bulky device out of his bag and shoved it into the pocket of his duffel coat, before placing his rucksack out of sight behind the sofa. 'Okay,' he said. 'I'm ready.'

The others pulled on their jackets and were getting ready to leave when there was an insistent rattle at the door. Through the glass, they saw Captain Tom outside.

'Captain Tom's never come to the beach hut before,' said Lucy, going to the door. 'I hope there's nothing wrong.'

When she opened the door, they could see straight away that something was very wrong. Captain Tom's usually bright and cheery face was creased with worry, and he wrung his cap anxiously in his hands. 'Have you seen Pugly?' he said at once. 'I was walking him along Gun Hill. I only looked away for a moment to buy a newspaper but when I turned back, he'd gone.' He looked at each of them in turn as though he had been hoping that they might have Pugly with them.

They all shook their heads. 'Sorry, Captain Tom,' said Lucy. 'We haven't seen him.'

Captain Tom stood in the doorway and looked

up and down the promenade anxiously. 'It's them dognappers,' he cried. 'I know it is. They've stolen poor Pugly. Oh heavens, what am I going to do? I couldn't bear it if I never saw him again.'

He ran his hand through his white hair until it stood up in wild spikes and his blue eyes filled with tears. The children felt desperately sorry for him, especially Charlie, who knew better than anyone what it would be like to lose a dog you loved more than anything in the world.

'Don't worry, Captain Tom,' she said. 'We'll help you find Pugly. Won't we, guys?'

The others agreed. They brought a shocked-looking Tom inside and sat him down, while Lucy poured him a cup of tea from the pot. 'Perhaps we should start with where you lost him,' said Joe. 'Did you see anything suspicious?'

Poor Tom stared into space and clutched his tea without drinking it. 'Nothing at all,' he said miserably. 'We were out early so there was hardly anyone about, just the postman on his bike and someone in a van on his way to work.'

'A van?' said Max. 'What did it look like?'

'I'm not sure,' said Tom. 'They all look the same to me. Why? D'you think it's important?'

'Oh, probably not,' said Max quickly. 'It's just useful to know if there were any witnesses in the area. Er... what colour did you say this van was?'

Captain Tom frowned in concentration. 'Er, I dunno... black, I think.'

The children looked at each other and Joe mouthed the words 'black van'. Captain Tom didn't seem to notice. He stood up, leaving his untouched cup of tea on the table.

'I can't sit around here while Pugly's missing,' he said miserably. 'I need to go and look for him.' He wrung his cap in his hands again. 'Oh, I know he's just an ugly little cross-eyed pug, but he means the world to me. If anything happened to him...' He tailed off, unable to finish his sentence.

'Perhaps you should go home and call the

police,' said Lucy kindly. 'They'll want a report as soon as possible.'

'And who knows, Pugly may have found his own way home by now,' added Charlie. 'Once when Sherlock ran away from me, he got home before I did.'

Captain Tom seemed to take some cheer from this news. 'Yes, yes, you're right,' he said. 'I should go home and see if he's there. Then I can call the police.'

The old man put on his cap and wandered out of the beach hut in a daze. He was so distracted that he even forgot to say goodbye and simply shuffled away in the direction of his house.

'Poor Captain Tom,' said Joe. 'He's really upset about Pugly.'

'Of course he is,' said Charlie. 'It's a terrible thing to lose your dog. We have to help him.'

'It's that black van again,' said Max. 'It's always somewhere in town, whenever anyone's dog goes missing. It has to be the dognappers.'

'If we hurry, we might still catch them,' said Lucy. 'We might even find Pugly.'

'Well, what are we waiting for,' said Joe. 'It's time for the After-School Detective Club to go into action.'

10

THE BLACK VAN

Filled with the urgency of a mission to save Pugly, the gang quickly got ready to leave. The activity woke Sherlock, who jumped up, tail wagging and excited to be going somewhere with his friends.

Charlie crouched down beside him and stroked his ears. 'I'm really sorry, Sherlock,' she said. 'But you can't come on this adventure. It's just not safe for you.'

Sherlock gave her a puzzled frown and cocked his head to one side, the way he did when he was being told something terribly important but had no idea what it was. Charlie poured him out some dog food and a bowl of water and made a comfortable nest of blankets for him to sleep in.

But even though she did everything possible to make him comfortable, she still felt miserable when they closed the door, especially when Sherlock looked out through the window with a bewildered expression. He simply could not understand why the gang was going somewhere without him.

Charlie insisted on watching Joe lock the door and she had to try the door handle several times before she was satisfied he had done it properly. Then with a last farewell wave to Sherlock, they were on their way.

They walked along the promenade, wearing serious expressions until they reached the pier. 'Maybe we should split up so we can search more quickly,' said Joe, who had seen enough TV shows to know the best way to search for a gang of ruthless criminals.

'I think we should stick together,' said Lucy. 'After all, we don't know who this gang is. They might be dangerous.'

'Perhaps we should go back for Sherlock,' said Charlie, looking back over her shoulder. 'He's not frightened of anything and I'm really worried about him being in that beach hut by himself.'

'No, we agreed,' said Max. 'He's safer where he is.' He pulled the artificial nose out of his pocket and pointed at the screen. 'See, he's right where we left him in the beach hut.' He put the device back in his pocket and then scanned the roads that led up the hill from the promenade. 'I suggest we stick together. We could walk up North Road and then down Pier Avenue and look along the side streets as we go.'

They agreed this was a good plan as all of them had felt secretly nervous about hunting for the dog thieves on their own. They started up the hill towards the top end of town, confident of success. They examined every parked vehicle, looked along side streets and even peered over hedges into people's driveways to see if they could catch a glimpse of the black van.

There was a moment's excitement when Joe spotted the hearse belonging to Mr Umbridge the undertaker. But no matter how much they squinted at it, they could not convince themselves it was the black van and they had to beat a hasty retreat when Mr Umbridge came out of his house and chased them away.

After an hour of fruitless searching, they had gone all the way to the top of the town and back to the promenade twice without seeing anything that looked like the dognappers' van. 'This is hopeless,' said Max, flopping down onto a bench. 'We haven't even searched half of the town yet. The dognappers could be miles away with Pugly by now.'

'Poor Pugly,' said Lucy, sitting beside Max. 'It's awful to think what might be happening to him.'

'I'm tired,' said Joe. 'And it's gone lunchtime.

Let's face it, we're never going to find this van.'

'I'm not so sure,' said Charlie. 'I think I can see it!'

Charlie had taken out her bird-spotting binoculars and was looking along one of the roads that led towards the top end of town. 'Look!' she cried. 'There it is.'

The others caught a brief glimpse of a black vehicle a long way up the hill, as it crossed the road and disappeared into a side street. 'It's probably just Mr Umbridge's hearse again,' said Max. 'He's not going to be very pleased if he finds us snooping around it a second time.'

'It looked like a taxi to me,' said Joe. 'Did it have a light on top of it?'

'Who's the one with the binoculars here?' snapped Charlie. 'It was a black van. The same one we saw the other day, I'm sure of it.' They were all squinting into the distance now, even though the vehicle had disappeared from view.

'So, what do we do now?' said Max nervously. Now they had spotted the dognappers' van, he suddenly didn't feel half as brave as he had done back in the beach hut.

'We said we were going to investigate,' said Charlie. 'So, that's what we should do. Now come on!'

Before anyone could argue, Charlie took off at a run, ducking across the road and up the hill towards the place where they had seen the van. Lucy and Joe sprinted after her, leaving Max standing alone.

'Great,' he muttered under his breath. 'Why does being a detective always have to involve so much running? I bet Sherlock Holmes never had this trouble.' He started after the others at a slow jog.

It took Max nearly five minutes to reach the top of the hill because he had to keep stopping to catch his breath. At one point, an old lady even came out of her house to make sure he was alright because he was leaning on her garden wall and gasping like a stranded fish.

When he finally caught up with his companions,

he found them crouched on a street corner, peering around a wall to look up a side street. 'It's the suspect vehicle,' hissed Joe in a stage whisper as Max arrived. 'I've made a positive ID.'

'"Suspect vehicle"?' said Max with a frown. '"Positive ID"? What are you talking about, Joe? This isn't a TV show. Is it the same van or not?'

'It looks like it,' said Charlie.

'But it's difficult to know for sure,' said Lucy. 'None of us got the numberplate before so we can't be certain.'

Max mopped the sweat off his brow with his handkerchief and frowned. 'Well, have you tried looking through the windows?' he said.

'It might be dangerous,' said Joe. 'What if the gang are all in the back and they decide to dognap us as well?'

Max rolled his eyes. 'All I want to do is look through the window,' he said. 'And besides, how many dognappers do you think could hide in there?' Now that he had jogged all the way to the top of the hill, Max was feeling hot and cross and a lot less anxious than he had before. All he wanted to do now was get this over with so he could go home for some lunch and a lie-down.

'We should go carefully,' said Lucy. 'And someone should stay here and keep watch. If anyone comes, they could give us a warning whistle.'

Joe volunteered to keep watch because this was also something he had seen done on TV and because he was the only one who could stick his fingers in his mouth and whistle. The others moved cautiously towards the black van, glancing guiltily over their shoulders as they went and looking extremely suspicious.

The van certainly looked like the same one they had seen before. It was black and shiny and had no markings on the outside to distinguish it. When they crept up to the passenger window and looked inside, there was nothing obviously suspicious but there was a clipboard lying on the front seat with some writing in faint pencil.

Charlie peered at it through the glass. 'I can't see it very well,' she said. 'But it looks like a list of addresses. All of them are here in Southwold.'

'I bet it's a list of dog owners,' said Max. 'The dognappers must be visiting each one in turn.'

'Let's look in the back,' said Lucy. 'There might be some more clues in there.'

The back windows were finished in black glass and were much more difficult to see through. Max pressed his face right up against the glass and cupped his hands around his eyes.

'What can you see?' said Charlie impatiently. 'Are there any dogs in there?'

'I don't think so,' said Max slowly. 'There's a few boxes and... wait a minute!'

'What is it?' said the girls.

'It's a basket,' said Max excitedly. 'Like a dog basket. And there's a blanket inside it. I think someone has definitely had a dog in the back of here.'

The others pressed their faces against the

window alongside Max to take a look. Charlie smacked her fist into her palm. 'That proves it,' she cried. 'The dognappers are using this van to get around. When they catch a dog, they put it in the back where no one can see them.

'I bet it's soundproofed too so no one can hear them barking,' said Max. 'This is the evidence we were looking for. We should call the police straight away.'

They were interrupted by a shrill whistle from the corner of the street and looked up to see Joe waving his arms frantically in their direction. 'That's the signal,' gasped Lucy. 'Quick, everyone hide!'

The three children looked around frantically before ducking into a nearby front garden and hiding behind a privet hedge. When Max raised his head to look out, he saw that Joe had disappeared. Then he saw someone walking quickly along the street towards them.

'There's someone coming,' whispered Max. 'Keep out of sight.'

The man wore a black sweatshirt with the hood up and he kept his head down so that Max couldn't see his face. 'He's going towards the van,' he hissed. Then he gasped. 'And he's got a dog with him.'

The two girls crowded next to Max to get a look at the man. It was difficult to get a good view through the privet hedge, but they could see that he was leading a yellow Labrador puppy on a piece of rope.

They held their breath as the man went to the back doors of the van and unlocked them. He placed his bag in the back then pulled on the lead until the puppy hopped up inside the van.

'He's stealing that puppy!' whispered Max urgently. 'What are we going to do?'

The man locked the back doors then went to the front and took out the clipboard, lying on the seat. He stood next to the van, consulting the list carefully.

'He's checking for his next victim,' said Lucy.

'We should definitely call the police.'

'They'll never get here in time,' said Charlie. 'He'll be miles away by the time they arrive. We have to stop him, now!'

Before the others could stop her, Charlie leaped from her hiding place and hopped over the hedge. Then she ran up behind the man and jumped onto his back, wrapping her legs tightly around him.

'Stop right there, dognapper!' she yelled.

The man gave a yelp of surprise and dropped his clipboard as he flailed his arms wildly. Charlie responded by grabbing the hood of his sweatshirt and pulling it down over his eyes so that he couldn't see. 'What are you waiting for?' she shouted. 'Come and give me a hand.'

Lucy vaulted the hedge and bent low to grab one of the man's legs while Max ran around and grabbed the other leg. The man clawed at his hood, trying to see who was attacking him but when he tried to move his legs, he lost his balance and sat down on the pavement, sending Charlie sprawling.

'Robbery, murder!' he shrieked. 'Somebody help me! Call the police!'

Max and Lucy let go of the man's legs and the three children exchanged astonished glances. They were not sure what they had been expecting the dognapper to do but they had never imagined he would start shouting for the police.

A moment later, there was a pounding of footsteps on the pavement behind them. 'Wait, wait, what are you doing?' It was Joe, looking red-faced and very worried. He pointed to the man on the ground, who was now trying to catch his breath. 'That's not a dognapper, it's Sanjay.'

'Who?' said Max, Lucy and Charlie together.

'He's Sanjay the plumber,' cried Joe. 'He came to our house last month to install the new washing machine.'

Sanjay looked around at the children and blinked. Then his eyes settled on Joe. 'Master Joe!' he cried.

'What is the meaning of this? And who are these children? Your mother will be most displeased when I tell her what has happened here.'

'I'm really sorry, Sanjay,' said Joe, looking deeply embarrassed. 'We didn't mean to attack you. It was a case of mistaken identity.'

Max climbed stiffly to his feet and brushed the dust off his duffel coat. 'Joe! If you knew who it was, why didn't you warn us?' he said angrily.

'I tried,' said Joe desperately. 'Didn't you see my signal?'

'Do you mean the *don't attack, it's only Sanjay* signal?' said Max. 'Strangely enough, I think I missed it.'

Lucy and Charlie were helping Sanjay to his feet and brushing him down. 'We're really very sorry,' said Lucy. 'We thought you were a dognapper.'

'Dognapper?' Sanjay looked puzzled. 'I am no dognapper. I'm just a plumber.'

'We know that *now*,' said Charlie, giving Joe an angry glare. 'But when we saw a strange van around town that we didn't know, we thought it was suspicious.'

'Suspicious?' Sanjay looked confused. 'But this is my new van.' He patted the paintwork proudly. 'I've only had it for a week.'

Max gave a pained expression. 'That explains why we've never seen it before,' he said.

'And then when we saw you putting a puppy in the back of the van,' said Lucy, 'we thought you were stealing it.'

'A puppy?' said Sanjay. 'Oh, you mean Jasmine. I got her to keep me company while I am working. I used to leave her at home when I went to a customer's house but with all these dognappings, I take her with me now.'

'We really are very sorry, Sanjay,' said Joe again. 'Can you forgive us?

Fortunately, Sanjay turned out to be a very good-natured plumber. After they had helped him up and brushed the rest of the dust from his clothes, he said he completely understood why they had mistaken him for a dognapper. He even unlocked the back of the van and let them pet Jasmine, who jumped up at them with big paws and covered them all with excitable licks.

After they had apologised once more, they waved goodbye as Sanjay and Jasmine drove away, then they stood in a forlorn group at the side of the road.

'Well, we made a real mess of that,' said Lucy.

'We really couldn't have got it any more wrong.'

'So much for our powers of detection,' said Max.

'And it means the dognappers are still out there somewhere,' said Lucy. 'And until we find them, no dog in Southwold is going to be safe.' She shivered and hugged herself tightly.

'We could keep looking, I suppose,' suggested Joe, but he didn't say it very enthusiastically.

'Well, I've had enough,' said Charlie. 'Right now, all I want to do is collect Sherlock and go home.'

They all agreed that the day had been a failure and that it was time to head back. They made their way back down the hill, thinking gloomy thoughts about dognappers and the embarrassing episode with Sanjay. But if they had thought that the day could not get any worse, then they were mistaken.

As they approached the beach hut, Charlie stopped in her tracks. 'Joe,' she said. 'I thought I told you to lock that door.'

'I did lock it,' complained Joe. 'You saw me do

it. You checked it yourself...' He tailed off in mid-sentence and stared in horror at the door of the beach hut, which was swinging in the breeze.

'Oh no,' gasped Charlie. 'Oh no, oh no, oh no.' She broke into a run and darted inside the hut. There was a brief pause and then she screamed.

'Sherlock!' she cried. 'He's not in here!'

The others ran to the hut and looked through the doorway. Charlie stood in the middle of the room with a face as white as a sheet, holding the blanket she had laid out for Sherlock to lie on. But the little dog was nowhere to be seen.

'He's gone!' wailed Charlie. 'The dognappers have taken Sherlock!'

11

SHERLOCK

Sherlock was unhappy.

The only time Charlie ever went anywhere without him was when she went to school. But she wasn't at school today and yet she had still left him behind in the beach hut.

Sherlock loved being with Charlie more than anything in the world. And he liked it best when she was with her friends, because he loved them almost as much as he loved her. They were kind, they always made a big fuss of him and, best of all, they always had a *lot* of food with them.

When Joe had locked the door to the beach hut, Sherlock had sprung up on a chair and pressed himself against the window. He barked to let them know they had made a mistake because he, Sherlock, was still inside. But then they began to walk away without him.

Sherlock's barking grew louder as the children got further away and he tried to make them hear him. He put his paws up against the window and continued barking until his doggy breath steamed the glass.

But it made no difference; Charlie and the others just continued walking. And even though he continued barking for a long time after they had disappeared from view, Charlie didn't come back.

When Sherlock had grown tired of barking, he spent some time looking out of the window and growling at the seagulls on the promenade. Sherlock and Charlie disagreed on the subject of seagulls. Sherlock had always regarded it as his duty to chase the annoying, squawky birds wherever he found them and Charlie seemed equally determined to stop him. Whenever he got the chance, there was nothing he liked nothing better than to run at a flock of seagulls, barking and snapping until they lumbered wheezily into the air and circled above him in a flock of noisy outrage.

Of course, Sherlock had never actually caught a seagull, and he had no idea what he would do with one if he did. All he knew was that chasing seagulls and making them scatter in panic was the best fun a small dog could have.

But today, no matter how much Sherlock barked at them, the seagulls refused to fly away. They looked up at him, trapped behind the windows of the beach hut, and considered him with their greedy yellow eyes. Then, when they had decided he was no threat, they went back to squabbling over empty crisp packets and discarded sandwich crusts.

Sherlock suspected they were laughing at him.

With a small doggy sigh, he got down from the window and ate some of the dog food from his bowl. Then he lay down on the blanket that Charlie had laid out for him, smelling her scent on the soft cloth as he closed his eyes.

Sherlock did not know how long he slept. He dreamed he was chasing seagulls on the beach, which somehow turned into sausages and then sprouted wings before flying away. Sherlock's legs twitched and he whined a little in his sleep as he snapped at the imaginary flying sausages, which always seemed to be just out of reach.

He woke to the sound of the beach hut door being opened and jumped up, tail wagging and instantly awake in the way that only dogs can be. Then he shrank back in surprise. A dark figure lunged at him from the bright doorway and a rough and smelly sack was dropped quickly over his head.

He barked furiously as a rough hand pinned him down and fumbled with the collar round his neck. Then he was scooped up in a wriggling bundle and someone shook the sack vigorously.

'We've got a lively one in here,' said a man's voice. The sack was shaken again, and he laughed as Sherlock responded furiously. 'Look at this,' he cried. 'This makes him really mad.'

'Stop messing around,' said a woman's voice. 'Just get him in the car while I see if there's anything else in here worth taking.'

Sherlock was puzzled. Who were these people? He didn't recognise their voices, but he knew they weren't meant to be in here. This place belonged to Charlie's friends.

The sack was carried outside. He could see daylight through the material, but he couldn't see what was going on. Then he heard the sound of a car boot being opened and there was a hard jolt as the sack was dropped roughly inside. When the boot slammed shut, there was darkness.

After a short while, the car started up and began to move. Sherlock was used to travelling in cars, but not in the boot where he couldn't see anything and certainly not inside a sack. The car accelerated hard and made sudden turns that made him roll around in the back until he felt sick. He wished Charlie was with him.

After a while, the car came to a stop and the sack was pulled roughly out of the boot. Sherlock felt himself being carried up a short flight of steps and then a door closed behind him and the sack was dropped onto the ground. He began barking again and snarling at his unseen attackers.

'That one sounds vicious,' said the woman's voice. 'We can't sell dogs that bite. Nobody wants 'em.'

'He's a terrier,' said the man. 'They're all like that. People pay good money for this sort of dog, trust me. Now get him into the crate with the others. We need to get them on the boat by this evening.'

'We're leaving this evening?' said the woman, surprised.

'We've got all we can from this place,' said the man. 'People are starting to ask questions.'

Sherlock didn't hear the rest of the conversation. The sack was lifted up again and he was carried into another room. He heard the sound of a padlock being undone and then he smelled something.

It was the smell of other dogs.

A great howling and yapping began, as though a dozen dogs had all come awake at the same time. Sherlock's sack was upended, and he tumbled into the open top of a large wooden crate. Before he had time to jump up again, the crate was slammed shut and he heard the sound of the padlock being snapped.

The howling continued all around him and he felt warm fur, moving in the darkness. As his eyes adjusted, he could make out several doggy shapes, crammed into the narrow crate. There was a Labrador, who Sherlock had seen before and who, he thought, was called Morrie. Two poodles he didn't know cowered in a corner and looked at him with frightened eyes. In another corner, a tiny Pekingese barked furiously and bared her little teeth while a big shaggy dog hid his head beneath his paws and whimpered softly.

Sherlock had never seen so many dogs in such a small space. He usually liked meeting other dogs, but these dogs all seemed too scared or angry to make friends right now. Poor Sherlock's tail sank between his legs, and he backed into a corner of the crate and sat down.

He decided he did not like this place. It was too

crowded and there was no fresh air or comfortable blankets to lie on. Nor was there any food to eat or even a bowl of fresh water to drink. More than anything, Sherlock wanted Charlie to come and take him home right now.

Then he spotted a small dog sitting on his own and looking very forlorn. It only took Sherlock a moment to recognise the stumpy tail, the squashed-up face and the funny crossed eyes. It was his friend Pugly.

The two dogs were overjoyed to see each other. They barked and yipped and licked each other's faces and sniffed each other thoroughly to show how glad they were to have found a friend in this awful place.

And when they had greeted each other properly, they lay together in a corner of the dark and smelly crate. Pugly placed his head on his paws and blinked his big eyes mournfully while Sherlock rested his head on Pugly's back.

Sherlock had no idea who had brought him to

this horrible place, but he was certain that Charlie would never have allowed it. He wondered what she was doing now and if she was missing him as terribly as he was missing her.

12

THE TRUTH COMES OUT

It took a long time to calm Charlie and stop her rushing straight out into the street to look for Sherlock. 'Let me go!' she screamed. 'They've got Sherlock. I have to go and search for him. We have to go the police. We have to organise a search party. We have to... we have to...' And finally, she broke down in tears and sobbed on Lucy's shoulder. 'I have to get him back,' she cried. 'I just have to.'

'You will,' said Lucy, trying to sound reassuring. 'Perhaps he hasn't been stolen. What if your mum came by and took him for a walk?'

'Mum never walks Sherlock,' said Charlie miserably. 'And besides, how could she get in? The door was locked.'

'That's a good point,' said Joe. 'I locked it myself. So how did the dognappers get in?'

Max bent down to inspect the front door. 'There's no signs of a break-in,' he said. 'No windows haven't been broken and the lock hasn't been forced. Are you sure you locked the door, Joe?'

'I'm *totally* sure,' insisted Joe.

Max stroked his chin thoughtfully, then stood up and clutched the lapels of his jacket, the way he did when he had something serious to say. *'When all other possibilities have been eliminated,'* he said importantly, *'whatever remains, however improbable, must be the truth.'*

'What are you on about now?' said Joe impatiently.

'It's what Sherlock Holmes says,' said Max. 'Look, we know that Joe locked the door, and the hut wasn't broken into. So, the only possible explanation is that someone must have let themselves in here with a key.'

'But I've got my key right here,' said Joe, holding it up. 'There's only two and the other one is...' He tailed off as realisation took hold.

'The other one is with Miranda Fitchwitherington,' said Max, finishing the sentence. 'She let herself in here before we arrived. She must have come back again after we left.'

'Miranda Fitchwitherington?' gasped Charlie. '*She* took Sherlock?' She pulled herself away from Lucy. 'Right, I'm going to find her. If she's harmed a hair on Sherlock's head I'll, I'll...'

'We need to calm down and think clearly,' said Lucy. 'I know we all hate Miranda but she's the daughter of a lord. She goes to our school. It doesn't make sense that she's the dognapper.'

'It's the only explanation that fits the facts,' said Max. 'She has the only other key, and she knew that Sherlock was here. Either she took him herself, or she gave the key to whoever did.'

Charlie punched her fist into her palm. 'I know she's behind this somehow,' she said angrily. 'Joe, do you know her address?'

Joe shrugged. 'No,' he said. 'The Fitchwitheringtons have been to our house lots of times, but I have no idea where they live.'

'Wait a minute.' Max smacked his palm against his forehead. 'I'm an idiot. I fitted one of my tracking collars to Sherlock before we went out. We can use the artificial nose to find out exactly where he is.'

'Brilliant, Max,' said Lucy. 'Do it now.'

'And please hurry,' added Charlie.

'I'm on it,' said Max. 'Let me just put on my reading glasses so I can see the screen better. Now, where did I leave my backpack?'

Joe bent down to pick up something up from the floor. 'Uh-oh,' he said. 'I'm not sure the tracking device you attached to Sherlock is going to be much use, Max,' he said.

'Why ever not?' said Lucy.

Joe held up an unbuckled dog collar. 'Because the dognappers took it off before they stole him.'

'Oh no,' gasped Lucy. 'That means we have no way of finding out where he is.'

'Hang on a minute,' said Max in a worried voice from behind the sofa. 'I can't find my backpack. I'm sure I left it here before we went out and now...' He turned around with a dismayed look on his face. 'Oh no, I think the dognappers took that too. My laptop was in it. What am I going to do? Mum will kill me.'

The four friends stared at each other in horror. 'Max, I'm so sorry,' said Lucy. 'What are we going to do now?'

'We're going to find Miranda Fitchwitherington,' snapped Charlie. 'She knows what happened to Sherlock and she probably took Max's backpack too.'

'But we still don't know where she lives,' insisted Joe.

'Maybe not,' said Charlie. 'But your mum must

know. Estate agents keep records of that sort of thing.'

'She's working at home today,' said Joe. 'She was making a list of more houses for Lord and Lady F to look at.'

'Well, what are we waiting for?' said Lucy. 'Let's go!'

They left immediately, pausing only long enough for Joe to lock the door even though, as he pointed out, there was nothing left inside worth stealing, then they set off in the direction of Joe's house at a steady run. As usual, Max quickly fell behind but even though he had a stich in his ribs, he didn't complain, because this was an emergency.

It took them nearly twenty minutes to reach Joe's house. By the time Max caught up, the others were gathered around the wide front gates, looking up the gravel drive towards Joe's house.

'Thanks... for waiting... guys,' wheezed Max as

he arrived. He bent over and leaned heavily on his knees as he gasped for breath.

Then he saw what they were all staring at.

Parked on the driveway in front of Joe's house was a large police car with a blue light on top. 'What are the police doing here? he said.

Joe blinked at the police car and swallowed. 'I-I don't know,' he said. 'Mum and Dad's cars are both here too. I don't understand it.'

'Well, if the police are already here, it saves us the bother of calling them,' said Charlie. 'As soon as we tell them what happened, they can go straight round to arrest the Fitchwitheringtons. Come on.'

They marched up the driveway and skirted around the empty police car. The front door was open, and Joe led them towards the sound of voices in the living room.

'Mum! Dad!' cried Joe as he burst through the living room door. 'We've been robbed. The dognappers broke into the beach hut and took Sherlock and Max's laptop. And, guess what? It was Miranda Fitchwitherington that did it. We have to stop them; we have to go round to their house and...'

He tailed off suddenly as he took in the scene in the room. His mother was perched on the edge of the sofa, dabbing her eyes with a handkerchief while Joe's dad stood behind her with a reassuring hand on her shoulder.

There was a police officer in uniform, sitting on a chair opposite Joe's mum. She had an open notebook on her lap and wore a serious expression. The other person was a tall man in a raincoat. He had steel-grey eyes and a kind expression and the children recognised him as the detective they had spoken to at the end of their first adventure together.

'Inspector Callahan,' said Joe. 'What are you doing here? Is everything alright?'

The inspector looked at Joe and frowned. 'Ah, young Joe, isn't it?' he said. He looked at the others as they squeezed around the door frame. 'I see you've brought the rest of the After-School Detective Club with you. I might have known that you lot wouldn't be far away when a serious crime has been committed.'

'A serious crime?' said Max. 'What's happened?'

'All of Mrs Carter's jewellery has been stolen

from the house,' said the woman police officer.

Penelope Carter started a fresh outbreak of wailing. 'They took everything,' she sobbed. 'My best earrings, my pearl necklace and even my favourite sapphire bracelet.'

'I don't suppose you lot know anything about this, do you?' said Inspector Callahan.

'Mum's jewellery?' said Joe. 'N-no, I don't know anything about that.'

'But somebody stole Charlie's dog, Sherlock,' said Lucy.

'And my laptop,' said Max.

'It was the Fitchwitheringtons,' snapped Charlie. 'They took my dog. I know they did.'

'Charlotte Wells, that's quite enough of that sort of talk,' said Joe's mother sternly. 'You can't go around accusing people like that. The Fitchwitheringtons are very important people.'

'Actually,' interrupted Inspector Callahan. 'I hate to break this to you, but Lord Fitchwitherington isn't who he claims to be.'

Joe's mother stared at the police inspector. 'He's not?'

'I'm afraid not,' said the inspector. 'I was about to explain when the children arrived. We've checked with the House of Lords and I'm afraid there is no record of anyone called Lord and Lady Fitchwitherington. We think they might be con artists.'

'Con artists?' said Penelope Carter. She said it as though the words tasted bad in her mouth. 'You've obviously made a mistake, officer. Lord Fitchwitherington is an educated man. He knows the king.'

'He drives a Bentley,' added Joe's dad.

Inspector Callahan consulted his notebook. 'The Bentley was stolen three weeks ago from a car dealer in Felixstowe,' he said. 'We think the Fitchwitheringtons might be the same gang that's been operating all over the country. It's the same each time: the father, mother and daughter turn up in a new town, pretending to be wealthy or related to royalty and saying they want to buy a house in the area. They enrol the daughter at the local school and they get an estate agent to show them around different houses so they can decide which ones to burgle.'

Penelope Carter gasped and placed her hand on her heart. 'An estate agent!' she wailed. 'Oh my. They said they wanted to settle down in Southwold. I showed them more than a dozen houses. I thought I was going to be employee of the month.' She started sobbing again and dabbed at her eyes before blowing her nose noisily.

'I was going to sell Lord Fitchwitherington our beach hut,' said Joe's dad in a shocked voice. 'I've already signed the papers and given him the keys.'

'Yes, we know about that,' said the inspector. 'It turns out that Lord Fitchwitherington was already trying to sell your beach hut to someone else. He's shown it to at least three different people who were interested in buying it.'

'What?' gasped Joe's dad. 'But he hasn't paid

me for it yet. Why, the rotten, thieving...'

'You mustn't blame yourselves, Mr and Mrs Carter,' said the inspector sympathetically. 'This is a professional gang and lots of people have been taken in by them. They're cunning people and they always manage to give us the slip just as we're about to close in on them.'

Charlie stamped her foot in frustration. 'I don't care about any stupid jewellery,' she cried. 'They took my dog. What are you going to do about that?'

The inspector's face became even more serious. 'The dog thefts only started quite recently,' he said. 'But we're pretty sure it's the same gang. We think they're stealing them to order and selling them to customers abroad. They've probably bribed someone to smuggle the dogs out of the country.'

Charlie turned pale. 'Selling them abroad?' she gasped. 'But that means I might never see Sherlock again.'

The inspector shook his head sadly. 'I'm sorry,'

he said. 'But unless we can catch the gang before they sell those dogs, we might never track them down.'

Charlie looked like she was about to say more but at that moment, the police officer's radio crackled to life. *'Officer Benton, are you receiving me?'* came the voice over the radio. *'I've got an urgent message about the Fitchwitherington case.'*

The police officer picked up her radio from the coffee table. 'Excuse me, Inspector,' she said. 'I need to take this call. I'll be outside if you need me.' She got up and slipped past the children into the hallway.

Poor Charlie's face had turned ashen. 'They're going to sell Sherlock,' she said in a small voice. 'But he belongs to me. I've had him since he was a puppy and we've never been apart before. I can't bear the thought of him being bought by someone else. I just can't...' She buried her face in her hands and began to sob as Lucy put an arm around her shoulder.

Everyone in the room looked unhappy for Charlie. The inspector gazed uncomfortably at his shoes and even Joe's mum looked upset. 'Isn't there something you can do to help Charlie find her dog, Inspector?' she said.

The inspector shook his head. 'We're looking for the gang right now,' he said. 'But, as usual, they're one step ahead of us. They left the bed and breakfast they were staying in this morning. I expect they're miles away by now.'

Just then there was a commotion in the hallway and the policewoman pushed her way back into the room, looking red-faced and anxious.

'Inspector!' she cried. 'That was the station. There's a lead on the case.'

'What sort of lead?' barked the Inspector.

'They've found a booking on the evening ferry from Felixstowe,' said the policewoman. 'Three tickets in the name of Archibald Fitchman, travelling with his wife and daughter.'

Inspector Callahan smacked a fist into his palm.

'Archibald Fitchman? That has to be them,' he cried. 'This could be our lucky break. What time does the ferry leave?'

'Six thirty, Inspector.'

The inspector checked his watch. 'Tell them to hold the ferry until we get there,' he said. He turned to Joe's mum and dad. 'Mr and Mrs Carter, could you come with us in the police car? We'll need someone who can identify the Fitchwitheringtons. Who knows, they might even have your jewellery with them.'

'My jewellery?' gasped Penelope. 'Do you really think so?'

'We'll happily come, Inspector,' said Joe's dad. 'Nothing would give me greater pleasure than to see them all behind bars.'

'What about us?' said Joe. 'We could help identify the gang too.'

'Well, I'm definitely coming,' said Charlie. 'I have to know if Sherlock's safe.'

'I'm sure we'd be helpful, Inspector,' added

Max. 'After all, I have read quite a lot of Sherlock Holmes stories.'

Everyone started talking at once and the inspector held up his hands for silence. 'Calm down, everyone,' he said, raising his voice above the noise. He looked at the children. 'I'm afraid there's no question of you lot coming along. This is police business and it could be dangerous. Besides, there's not enough room for all of you in the police car. You'll have to stay here. You'll find out soon enough if we've caught the gang.'

He ignored the howls of protest from Charlie, Lucy, Max and Joe and gathered up his coat. 'I won't hear any more about it,' he said sternly. 'Now then, Mr and Mrs Carter, if you're ready?'

The children watched with dismay as Joe's mum and dad collected their coats and followed the two police officers outside to the car. 'Don't look so unhappy, darling,' said Penelope Carter as she bent down to kiss Joe on the cheek. 'Just wait here patiently with your friends until we get back.'

She gave the three friends a disapproving glance. 'Better take them in the TV room, though,' she said in a loud whisper. 'They look a bit grubby to be sitting on my living-room sofas.'

Before Joe could object, Penelope Carter had climbed into the back of the police car, next to her husband, and the police car started to pull out of their drive. As the car accelerated away up the road, the driver turned on the blue flashing lights and the sirens.

'Well, how d'you like that,' said Max, as the sirens receded into the distance. 'After all we've done for the police, you'd think they'd take us along with them.'

'It's so unfair,' cried Charlie. 'He's my dog and he's a hundred times more important than any stolen jewellery.'

'We might as well face it,' said Lucy. 'We're just going to have to wait this one out.'

13

THE DECOY

Having got over the disappointment of being left behind, Max realised that he was both thirsty and starving hungry.

'How about a sandwich and a cup of tea, Joe?' he said. 'What with all that running around earlier, we didn't get any lunch.'

Charlie said she didn't feel like eating anything, but the others thought it was a good idea and Joe led them all into the kitchen and put on the kettle.

The kitchen in Joe's house was like something out of a spaceship. Max stared at a machine finished in bright chrome and bristling with dials, pipes and blinking lights. 'What does this thing do?' he said. 'It looks like a steam engine.'

'It's a coffee machine,' said Joe absently. 'My dad said it's the best cappuccino maker that money can buy.'

'Can we try it?' said Max eagerly.

Joe shook his head. 'Not really,' he said. 'We've never been able to figure out how it worked. We've got instant coffee if you want?'

Max made a face. 'I'll just stick with tea, thanks.' He peered at another machine that looked like a giant clamshell made of metal. 'What about this?' he said, opening the lid experimentally. 'What does this do?'

'Toasted sandwich maker,' said Joe with a grin. 'Makes perfect toasties in two minutes, every time.'

'Now you're talking,' said Max, rubbing his hands together. 'How about a melted cheese toastie?'

'How can you talk about food when Sherlock's still missing?' snapped Charlie. 'Aren't you worried about him?'

Joe and Max looked down at their feet sheepishly. 'Sorry, Charlie,' said Max. 'I *am* really worried about Sherlock but I'm also really hungry. You know I can't think straight when I'm hungry.'

Charlie glared at Max but Lucy intervened. 'I think what Max means,' she said, 'is that there's nothing else we can do to help Sherlock right now. The best thing we can do is all have a rest and a cup of tea and wait for news. I have to say those sandwiches sound pretty good too.'

'Coming right up,' said Joe, who liked nothing better than the opportunity to show off what he could do in the kitchen.

Charlie did not look convinced, but she accepted a cup of tea from Joe and sat down at the kitchen table. 'I feel so useless sitting here,' she said. 'I can't stand all this waiting.'

No sooner had she spoken than there was a loud rumbling from outside that shook the glass in the windowpanes as something large and heavy crunched its way up the gravel drive.

'Now, who's that?' said Joe, placing a plate full of toasted sandwiches down on the table. 'Surely it's not the police car back from Felixstowe already?'

They rushed to the window and looked out to see an ancient motorcycle and sidecar rumbling up the driveway. The motorbike pulled to a halt and backfired noisily, scaring a flock of birds into the air from the nearby apple tree.

'It's Captain Tom,' said Lucy. 'And he's brought *The Thunderer.*'

They hurried outside, where Captain Tom was dismounting the ancient motorbike and removing his helmet and goggles. 'Captain Tom, it's nice to see you,' said Joe, eying the old bike enviously. 'What are you doing here?'

The captain tucked the helmet under his arm and gave them a nod. 'Good to see you too, young folks,' he said. 'I just thought I'd stop by and see if you'd heard anything about the dognappers? There was a rumour in town that there was a police car parked in your driveway this morning.'

'People don't miss much around here, do they?' said Max.

'There *was* a police car here,' said Lucy. 'They think the Fitchwitheringtons are the dognappers.'

'They took all of Mum's jewellery too,' said Joe. 'The police took Mum and Dad to Felixstowe to see if they could catch them.'

'Did they indeed?' said Captain Tom. 'Well, that's good news, I suppose.' Then he sighed. 'But I was hoping there might be some news of Pugly. It's just not the same without the little feller around the house.'

He looked so unhappy that the children all felt sorry for him. 'Come inside and have a cup of tea, Captain Tom,' said Joe. 'It will make you feel better.'

The captain accepted gratefully, and they all trooped back inside the house. When they were all seated at the kitchen table with fresh mugs of tea in front of them, Captain Tom turned to Charlie.

'I heard the dognappers took your Sherlock too,' he said. 'It's a terrible thing to take someone's dog.

A dog is like a member of your family. Losing a dog is like losing a person.'

Charlie nodded glumly. 'That's how I feel too,' she said in a small voice. A large tear spilled out of the corner of her eye and rolled down her face. 'I don't think I could bear it if I never found him again.'

Captain Tom smiled kindly. 'Well, don't you worry yourself about that, young Charlie,' he said. 'Because dogs are clever, you see. If a dog gets separated from the person they love most, they'll stop at nothing to find them again. Why, I've heard of dogs finding their way home from more than a hundred miles away.' He patted Charlie on the hand. 'Sherlock's a smart dog. If there's any way for him to get back to you, then he'll find it. Believe me.'

Charlie smiled. 'Thanks, Captain Tom,' she said.

'What about Pugly?' said Joe. 'Do you think he'll find his way home too?'

The captain scratched his long white beard.

'I dunno,' he said. 'The thing is, Pugly is as stupid as a tin of beans. But I'm sure if he's with Sherlock he'll be alright.' He sighed again. 'I just wish we knew where they both were.'

'I made tracking collars for both of them,' said Max miserably. 'But they took Sherlock's collar off before they stole him, and I never got a chance to give Pugly his.'

Captain Tom nodded. 'Well, that sounds very clever, young Max,' he said. 'Don't you worry, I'm sure you'll be able to give it to him at some point.'

Max shook his head. 'I don't think so,' he said. 'You see, Pugly's collar was in my bag with my laptop and the dognappers stole it.'

As soon as he finished his sentence, Max suddenly sat bolt upright as though somebody had given him an electric shock. Then he slapped his forehead with his hand. 'Wait a minute,' he said. 'I totally forgot. The collar I made for Pugly is still in my bag.'

Joe frowned. 'How does that help us? The

dognappers took it and they're probably miles away by n—' He stopped in mid-sentence and his eyes opened wide. 'Oh, wait,' he said. 'I get it!'

'Get what?' said Captain Tom. 'What are you youngsters talking about?'

'The tracking collar I made for Pugly is still in my backpack,' explained Max, patiently. 'That means I can track it using the artificial nose.'

'Artificial *what?*' said Captain Tom. 'Have you taken leave of your senses, young Max?'

Max fumbled in the pocket of his duffel coat and pulled out the clunky device he had shown the others earlier. 'This is my artificial nose,' he said. 'It can follow the trail of the dognappers wherever they go.'

'Max, that's brilliant,' said Lucy. 'Do you think it's still working?'

'The battery should last six weeks,' said Max as he tapped instructions into the device. 'As long as they haven't thrown it away, we should be able to see exactly where they are.'

'We already know where they are,' said Joe. 'They're in Felixstowe, waiting to catch the evening ferry.'

Max thought for a moment. 'Well, I guess it doesn't do any harm to check,' he said. 'We might be able to give the police a precise location.'

The others leaned in around the table to watch

as a map appeared on Max's device. In the centre of the screen, a blue dot was pulsing its way along one of the main roads. 'Wow,' cried Joe. 'It's like watching a real-life police drama!'

Max frowned. 'Something's not quite right here,' he said. 'That's the signal from the collar alright. But the dognappers aren't in Felixstowe; they're headed in the other direction altogether.' He followed the road with his finger. 'Looking at this, I'd say they were on their way to Lowestoft.'

'That's a completely different port,' said Lucy.

'You mean the police have gone to the wrong place?' said Captain Tom.

'It's a decoy!' cried Joe. 'They must have booked ferry tickets to make the police think they were leaving from there.'

'And all the while they're heading in the other direction,' said Lucy.

'But that means the police won't find them,' cried Charlie. 'What are we going to do?'

'What can we do?' said Joe. 'The police have

gone, and we've got no way of getting to Lowestoft.'

Captain Tom cleared his throat. 'No way of getting to Lowestoft?' he said. 'That's where you're wrong, young Joe. We've got *The Thunderer*.'

The four children stared at Captain Tom. 'You mean your motorbike?' said Lucy.

'The one that's about a hundred years old?' said Max.

'We'd never all fit in it,' said Joe. 'Would we?'

'Certainly, we would,' said Captain Tom. 'My sidecar is licensed to carry three passengers and I can take one of you on the pillion seat.'

'Isn't that a little... risky?' said Max nervously.

Captain Tom gave Max a stern look. 'I'll have you know, young Max, that *The Thunderer* is in first-class mechanical condition, and I've got enough helmets for all of you. So, the only question is... are you bold enough?'

It was Charlie who answered first. 'Well, I am,' she said. 'If there's a chance of finding Sherlock I'll do it, whatever the risks.'

'Spoken like a true dog-lover,' said the captain. 'Well, if we're all done with talking, let's get moving. It's time we got on the trail of those dastardly dognappers and put 'em behind bars, once and for all.'

14

SHERLOCK'S PLAN

All the dogs looked very unhappy. Most lay on the floor of the crate, with their tongues hanging out, making little whining noises in the darkness. Sherlock thought of his water bowl at home, which Charlie always kept filled with fresh, cool water. He licked his lips as he imagined dunking his nose and lapping up greedy mouthfuls.

The two poodles had made themselves as small as possible in one corner, whilst Morrie the Labrador had curled up and was whimpering softly in his sleep. The little Pekingese just glared angrily at any dog that came near her and bared her needle-sharp teeth.

After a short while, Sherlock heard noises outside. The crate shuddered and tipped suddenly to one side as it was dragged across the floor. The dogs, who had been quite subdued, began yelping and barking again as they slid around inside until someone banged on the wooden walls.

'Shut that noise in there, can't you?' shouted an angry voice. 'Come on, let's get 'em in the van, quick before they attract suspicion.'

The crate was bumped down several stairs and then there was more crashing as it was lifted up and manhandled into a narrow space where the air smelled old and greasy. 'Blimey, those dogs is heavy,' said the man.

'Stop your complaining,' said the woman in an unpleasant tone. 'It was your idea, to start stealing dogs. I said we should stick to burglary. Dogs are more trouble than they're worth.'

'I told you, there's good money in dogs,' said the man. 'Now, where's that girl got to? Our boat leaves from Lowestoft in an hour.'

'I'm right here, Dad,' said a third voice. 'Keep your hair on, we've got plenty of time.'

As soon as Sherlock heard the girl's voice, his ears pricked up and he growled. He knew the voice belonged to that girl who had upset Charlie and her friends and who he disliked so much. She must be the one who had taken him away from Charlie.

He jumped up and began barking and scratching at the side of the crate until someone banged on it, only inches from his nose. 'Shut

up, you little beast,' the girl shouted. 'Or I'll throw you overboard when we get out to sea.'

Before Sherlock could protest any more, the doors to the van were slammed shut and the vehicle pulled away, sending all the dogs tumbling over each other again. There was an outbreak of snarling when Morrie accidentally sat down on the Pekingese but eventually, everyone settled down again as the van rumbled down the road.

They were on the move again.

Unlike the journey Sherlock had taken in the boot of the car, the van seemed to move much more slowly and Sherlock wondered how much longer they would have to be in here. He stretched his legs uncomfortably. He would have done anything for a run on the beach right now.

To pass the time, he began to sniff around the edges of the crate, using his sensitive doggy nose to investigate the more interesting details. Sherlock was good at sniffing things, and he could never understand why Charlie didn't seem to care about smells when they went on their walks. Instead of snuffling along close to the ground like him, she would turn her face up to the breeze where there were hardly any smells at all.

Sherlock, on the other hand, knew where all the best smells were kept. He would hoover his way along the pavements with his nose firmly on the ground, whiffling around the bottom of lamp posts, sniffing at rubbish bags and stopping to take a really good snuffle at anything that smelled like seagull.

But there was nothing in the crate that smelled remotely of seagull. Most of what he could smell was something that should have been safely buried in the back garden. The other dogs all smelled like they needed a good bath, except for the Pekingese, who smelled of flowers. Sherlock had never met a dog that smelled of flowers before and he went back for a second sniff. But she bared her tiny teeth at him again and he backed away carefully.

Then, he smelled something new. In one corner of the crate, the air smelled slightly fresher and cooler, and he felt a slight breeze on the end of his nose. He sniffed again. There was no doubt about it: fresh air was coming in from the outside. And if fresh air could get in... then maybe a dog could get out.

He pushed his nose into the corner until he felt one of the planks move. He pushed against the loose board and it moved again and, for a moment, his nose was right outside the crate.

Then Sherlock stuck his two front paws into the corner of the crate and began to scrabble at the boards, the way he did when he was trying to dig for rabbits. Pugly came and stood next to him and Morrie the Labrador looked over Pugly's shoulder. As Sherlock worked at the loose plank, all the other dogs became interested in what he was doing, except for the Pekingese, who turned her back as if the whole thing was beneath her.

Just when he was starting to get somewhere,

the van came to a sudden stop, sending Pugly face-first into Sherlock's backside. There was more howling and barking as Morrie got into an argument with the two poodles and the big shaggy dog cowered in a corner to get away from the Pekingese after he accidentally trod on her paw.

Moments later, the van doors opened again, and the crate was hauled outside. Sherlock sniffed the unmistakeable smells of the sea and diesel engines and heard the sound of seagulls. It smelled and sounded just like the harbour in Southwold, except that he could hear men shouting, and machinery lifting heavy boxes. This was a much bigger harbour than he had ever been in before.

Something rattled the crate and he heard metal shackles being locked into place. Then, without warning, the crate lurched and wobbled and began to swing violently.

All the dogs howled as the crate swung from side to side. Sherlock pressed his nose against the hole in the crate and gave a little yelp of surprise. The crate was moving through the air. Sherlock could not imagine how the box was flying. Could it be something to do with the seagulls?

The crate changed direction, and swung across the water and then down towards the deck of a large boat. Sherlock had been on boats before, but the boats he had been on were small and they had comfortable cushions where a dog could lie down and have a sleep if he wanted one. But this boat was big and ugly and streaked with rust. The decks were made of hard metal and there were no cushions in sight.

The moving crate came to a stop above the ship and swung gently for a few moments before starting to descend. Directly underneath them was a square hole in the deck, which seemed to be very black and very deep and smelled of old fish. Sherlock gave a small whine as he realised that they were about to be swallowed up.

The crate dropped lower and lower until the

darkness closed over it and the last chinks of daylight from outside disappeared. And poor Sherlock, realising that he might never see Charlie again, threw back his head and howled as though his doggy heart would break.

15

THE ROAD TO LOWESTOFT

Getting on board *The Thunderer* was a more complicated affair than any of them had imagined. Firstly, Captain Tom fetched the spare helmets from the sidecar and handed them around. The helmets were old-fashioned and battered and Joe peered into his dubiously.

'Er... Captain Tom, it looks like something has been *living* in here,' he said.

The captain looked into Joe's helmet and pulled out a clump of dried grass. 'That ain't nothing but an old mouse's nest,' he said matter-of-factly. 'I don't think there's anything in there right now, but give it a good shake out before you put it on to be on the safe side.'

Both Lucy and Charlie looked quite stylish in their helmets and goggles, but Max's was several sizes too small and he had to pull it over his head with the help of Joe, who pushed down from the outside. 'How's that?' enquired Joe when the helmet was in place.

'My ears are folded over,' replied Max in a loud voice. 'I can't hear anything!'

Once Captain Tom had checked that the helmets were all safely fastened, he showed them where to sit.

'Charlie and Joe, you can sit next to each other in the front of the sidecar,' he said. 'Just remember when we go round corners that you have to lean in the opposite direction, or we might topple over.'

'Is he serious?' whispered Joe to Charlie. 'My mum would have a hissy fit if she saw what I was doing right now.'

'Just shut up and get in,' said Charlie. 'It's our best chance of finding Sherlock.'

'Lucy, you're the tallest so you can ride pillion behind me.'

Lucy grinned at the prospect of riding on the back of the motorbike. She gave Tom a mock-salute. 'Ay-aye, Captain,' she said as she clambered on the back of the bike and rested her feet on the footrests.

'What about me?' said Max, looking at the sidecar uncertainly. 'There isn't room for me in there as well.'

'That's where you're wrong, young Max,' said the Captain. 'You're the lucky one because you get to go in the jump seat.'

'What did he say?' said Max, looking at the others. 'I can't hear a thing with this helmet on.'

The captain went to the rear of the sidecar and unfastened a small hatch that opened up to reveal a tiny seat, upholstered in red leather. Max frowned at the precarious little chair.

'Er... it's tiny,' he said. 'And it sort of hangs over the back. Are you sure it's safe?'

'Just get in,' barked Charlie. 'While you're arguing, the dognappers are getting further away.'

Still grumbling, Max hoisted himself into the jump seat with the help of Captain Tom. He fastened the small lap belt and pulled it tight, then he gripped the sides of the chair and looked down nervously. 'I'm dangling over the road,' he wailed.

'Oh, you'll get used to it,' said the captain cheerfully. 'Pugly loves sitting in that seat. Just remember to duck your head if we go under any low bridges.'

Max's eyes widened and he turned to look at Lucy. 'What did he just say?'

Lucy grinned. 'Don't worry about it,' she said. 'Get the artificial nose out. You'll need it to give the captain directions.'

Max fished the heavy device from his pocket and extended the aerial so that it jiggled around above his head. When he looked down at the screen, it made him feel calmer and it took his mind off how nervous he was feeling. 'They're still heading north,' he said, tracking the blue blob with his finger. 'But they're a long way ahead of us.'

'Don't you worry,' said the captain as he swung his leg over the saddle in front of Lucy. 'When I was a young man, I used to race my friends up the Lowestoft Road. I know every twist and turn.

189

Now, hold on to your hats, ladies and gentlemen.'

Captain Tom stamped down on the kick-starter with his heavy boot. It took two or three goes but then the engine burst to life with a noise like a tiger that has just been woken up by a prod with a sharp stick.

Captain Tom revved the engine several times and a cloud of blue smoke rose from the exhaust pipe, filling the air with the smell of hot oil. The ancient motorbike sounded ten times louder when they were actually sitting on it. The metal frame shuddered and vibrated their bones so that their teeth chattered in their heads and they had to shout to be heard.

'T-t-t-t-t-t-t-urn l-l-l-l-left. Out of the d-d-d-d-driveway!' yelled Max over the din.

'What did he say?' yelled Captain Tom.

'Left!' shouted the others in unison.

'Right-ho!' The old motorbike pulled away sharply, sending up a spray of gravel behind it. All the children clung to their seats, apart from Lucy, who had to hold on to the back of Captain Tom's leather overcoat.

When the motorbike started moving, the sound of the engine was overtaken by the roar of the wind. It wasn't so bad for Lucy, who was behind the captain, or for Charlie and Joe, who could crouch behind a tiny windshield. But up on the jump seat, Max got the full force of the wind in his face. The goggles protected his eyes but the fast-moving air made his cheeks wobble and forced his mouth into a terrified grimace.

They had gone nearly a mile when Joe cried out, 'Oh, no! In the excitement I forgot to leave Mum a message to say where we were going,' he yelled. 'I meant to tell her that the police are looking in the wrong place. I'd better call her.'

He pulled out his phone, which was a challenge because he was so tightly wedged against Charlie. Then he took several goes to dial the number because he was jiggling around so much.

Unfortunately, Joe had not considered how

he was going to speak to his mum while he was wearing a crash helmet. He clamped the phone to the side of the helmet hopefully and heard the faint strains of his mother's voice.

'Joe? ... Is that you... hardly hear you. Is that the washing machine?'

'Mum!' shouted Joe. 'I'm on a motorbike!'

'You're on a what? A *mountain hike?* Don't be ridiculous; there aren't any mountains in Southwold.'

'No, Mum. I'm outside on *The Thunderer!*'

'You're outside in your underwear? For heaven's sake, Joe. What will the neighbours say?'

'You have to listen, Mum,' yelled Joe at the top of his voice. 'Tell the police they're looking in the wrong place. They need to go to *arrgh...*'

At that moment, *The Thunderer* ran over a large bump in the road and the children all shrieked as their bottoms lifted off the seats. The motorbike slammed back down onto the tarmac, bouncing on its old springs, and the jolt jerked the phone from Joe's hand, sending it clattering away behind them.

'My phone!' he cried. 'We have to go back!'

'No time!' yelled Max. 'The dognappers are nearly in Lowestoft.'

'Don't you worry,' yelled the captain. 'The Lowestoft Road is coming up. Now I can show you what the old girl can do.'

The houses of Southwold fell away behind them and they were on the open road, running between low hedges. As soon as they were clear of traffic, Captain Tom opened the throttle and the acceleration pushed them back into their seats.

Captain Tom gunned the old motorbike through narrow lanes and sleepy villages, past cosy-looking pubs and war memorials and little thatched cottages with smoke curling from their chimneys. His bushy beard streamed behind him in the breeze, and he wore a huge grin. 'By thunder, this takes me back!' he cried. 'I haven't done a run like this in years.'

By now, the four friends were getting used to the noise and the wind and were even starting to enjoy the ride. Max reached into his pocket and pulled out something squashed and greasy. 'Does anyone want a cheese toastie?' he said cheerfully, holding out the battered sandwich. 'I picked up a few before we left the house.'

'Don't you think of anything but your stomach?' shouted Charlie. 'We're on a life-or-death mission here.'

'Balanced nutrition is essential for every crime fighter,' yelled Max. 'I can't be expected to be at the peak of genius if my tummy's rumbling.'

Joe turned in his seat and inspected the sandwich. 'Max, it's got something sticking to it,' he said, wrinkling his nose.

'It's just a wine gum,' said Max. 'I've got some of those in my pocket too if you'd prefer?'

Joe shook his head. 'Thanks, but I'm okay.'

Captain Tom slowed down as the countryside gave way to the outskirts of the town. 'The blue dot hasn't moved for some time,' yelled Max. 'I think they might have stopped in the dockyards.'

'Maybe they just dumped your bag,' said Charlie. 'Have you thought of that? We might get there to find your tracking device in a rubbish bin.'

'There's only one way to find out,' said Max. 'Head for the docks.'

They motored along the wide seafront, where tall houses with flaking paint faced a long, flat beach. As they approached the centre of town, they could see the rough concrete walls of the harbour, reaching out into a grey sea. A steady stream of boats in different sizes moved in and out of the harbour, ranging from tiny white dinghies to larger and more serious working ships painted in greys and greens.

'They're on the other side of the harbour,' yelled Max. 'We'll need to cross at the bridge.' He pointed to a low bridge ahead of them that spanned the harbour entrance. There were traffic lights either side of the bridge and steel barriers, which were in the upright position.

'They raise the bridge when a big ship needs to pass through the harbour,' said Captain Tom. 'It's a good job the bridge is down now or we'd have to wait.'

Joe's eyes widened. 'They raise the bridge?' he said. 'That's amazing. Can we stop and watch?'

Charlie smacked Joe around the back of his helmet. 'Stay focused, Joe,' she said. 'We haven't got time to wait until the bridge opens. You can be a tourist another day.'

'I'm not so sure,' said Lucy. 'It looks like Joe's about to get his wish. Look!'

The lights on the bridge started flashing red and a klaxon began blaring noisily. Up ahead, the traffic approaching the bridge was slowing to a stop and was forming a queue.

'They're going to raise the bridge now,' cried Max. 'We'll have to stop.'

'Not today, young Max,' barked Captain Tom. He pulled on the handlebars and the bike swerved around the traffic and headed down the centre of the road.

'Is he planning what I think he's planning?' gasped Max.

The motorbike reached the front of the queue and everyone held their breath as they rumbled onto the bridge. Captain Tom didn't stop; he opened the throttle and the old bike raced towards the far side.

Max looked up and gasped. 'Captain Tom!' he shrieked. 'The barriers are coming down.'

They saw it was true. On the far side of the bridge, the barriers had started to descend. Captain Tom crouched low behind the windscreen. 'Too late to back out now!' he cried.

As they roared across the bridge, Max could not take his eyes off the descending barrier. It seemed that they would arrive at the far side just in time for the heavy steel to come crashing down on his head. He opened his mouth to scream but, at the last moment, the bike gave

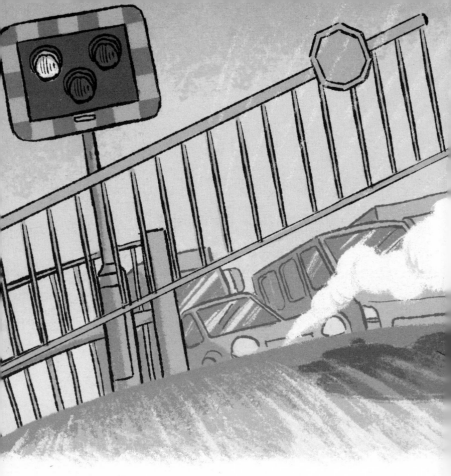

an extra burst of speed and they shot beneath the barrier an instant before it clanged to the ground.

'Woo-hoo!' yelled Joe, punching his fist in the air. 'That was brilliant, Captain Tom. Just like in the movies.'

'Aye,' said Tom, patting *The Thunderer*

affectionately. 'The old girl has plenty of fight left in her yet.'

Joe's eyes were shining. 'Can we go back and do it again?' he said.

'Can I remind everyone this isn't a joy ride,' said Charlie angrily. 'Max, do your job. You're supposed to tell us where the dognappers are.'

Max was looking back at the bridge, which was now rising into the air like a castle drawbridge. He gave a shudder at their narrow escape and then looked back at the device in his hand.

'Turn left here,' he gasped. 'They're somewhere in the inner harbour.'

Captain Tom turned off the main road into a large, gated entrance. A man with a peaked cap and a clipboard stepped out of a sentry box and held up his hand. When he saw the heavily laden motorbike, he scowled so deeply that his eyebrows knitted together in a thick hedge.

'And who might you be?' he said.

'We're the After-School Detective Club,' said Joe cheerfully.

'We're on a mission to catch the dognappers,' said Charlie.

'They're hiding out in your harbour,' added Lucy.

The man tilted back his head so he could look at them under the peak of his cap. 'Detective Club?'

he said. 'Dognappers? What kind of nonsense is this?'

'It's not nonsense,' said Max. 'We tracked them here using the artificial nose.' He coughed. 'Actually, it's my own genius invention.'

The man took a pencil from his pocket and wrote something on his clipboard. 'Well, genius or not, you're not coming in here. It's authorised vehicles only beyond this point, and this' – he tapped on The Thunderer's fuel tank with his pencil – 'is not an authorised vehicle.' He grinned triumphantly. 'That's maritime law, that is.'

Captain Tom glowered at the man. 'Maritime law?' he said. 'I'll have you know, young man, I was the lighthouse keeper at Southwold for nigh on thirty years and I know a thing or two about maritime law. For example, I know it's an offence to smuggle stolen canines out of the country.'

The man swallowed. 'Stolen canines?' he croaked.

'Dogs!' snapped Captain Tom. 'They've got my Pugly.'

'And my Sherlock!' added Charlie.

'And my laptop,' said Max.

'So, you see,' said Captain Tom. 'If you try and stop us, you'll be guilty of assisting an act of piracy on the high seas.'

'P-piracy?' stammered the man.

'Now, stand aside!' shouted Tom.

The man barely had time to jump clear as the motorbike pulled away with a jerk. Max looked back to see him waving his clipboard angrily in the air.

'I don't think that will hold him off for long,' said Lucy. 'He's bound to come looking for us.'

'We don't need to hold him off for long,' said Captain Tom. 'Where to now, young Max?'

'Turn left here,' shouted Max. 'They're somewhere in this area.'

The Thunderer turned between two low buildings and came to a halt on a concrete dock. Along the quayside, a dozen working ships were moored to iron bollards with stout ropes. Forklift trucks bleeped noisily as they manoeuvred crates along the jetties and a heavy crane was lifting containers into the hold of a large cargo vessel.

Out on the water, more working boats chugged noisily through the murky waters and everywhere they looked, men and women in hard hats were lifting boxes, securing cargoes and checking mooring lines.

There wasn't a single dog in sight.

'Well, where next?' said Charlie. 'Where are they?'

Max stared at the screen helplessly. 'I don't know,' he cried. 'The tracker isn't accurate enough to tell me. All I know is that they're somewhere in this harbour.'

Charlie stood up in the sidecar and looked around desperately. 'What use is that?' she cried. 'There's dozens of boats here and Sherlock could be in any one of them. We'll never have time to search them all.'

As they clambered off the bike and removed their helmets, Charlie looked desperately up and down the quayside. She ran, first in one direction and then in the other, trying to work out where her beloved pet might be.

And in the end, she just stood on the dock and cried out loud. 'Sherlock!' she sobbed. 'It's me, Charlie. Where are you, Sherlock?'

16

ESCAPE!

Silence had fallen over the crate as they dropped into the darkened hold of the ship. Sherlock lay in his corner with his head on his paws, wondering whether he would ever see Charlie again.

He felt so sad that he barely noticed when Pugly shuffled over wheezily to lick the end of his nose. All he could think about was Charlie and how she always knew just the right time to go for a walk or how she always had something tasty in one of her pockets or how he could always hear her voice when she called him, no matter how far away she was.

'Sherlock!'

Sherlock raised his head from his paws and blinked. Had he been thinking about Charlie so much that he'd imagined he could hear her?

He heard the voice again.

She sounded a long way off, and her voice barely carried over the noises of the boat and the sea and wind. But there could be no mistake.

It was Charlie. And she was calling his name.

He began to bark, louder and longer than he had ever barked in his life. He leaped at the sides of the crate, scratching against the wood with his claws in his desperation to get out.

The other dogs picked up on Sherlock's excitement and they began barking too, drowning out any possibility of hearing Charlie again. But Sherlock didn't care. Now he knew that Charlie was somewhere out there, and she was looking for him. That was all he needed to know.

But, if he was going to get to Charlie, he had to get out of this crate first. He returned to the corner and began scrabbling at the loose plank with renewed energy. He pulled it with his claws, chewed at it with his teeth and pushed his snout into the gap to try and make it wider.

And then it happened.

With a sudden crack, the old wood splintered and broke and a piece of the crate fell away. Sherlock pushed his snout into the hole and this time his whole head went through the gap. He wriggled and pushed with his back legs, forcing his shoulders through the narrow opening and breaking more of the wood in the process.

And then he was out! He pulled his body free of the hole and stood up, shaking himself thoroughly, the way he did when he came out of the sea. He blinked in the darkness and looked around.

The place he was standing in was dark and damp. The walls and floor were made of hard metal and a pool of greasy water had formed where he was standing. Stacks of crates were arranged around the walls and lashed down with heavy ropes. There were rusted oil drums, dirty rags and disused pieces of rope lying about. It looked like the sort of place where people didn't come very often and certainly not somewhere you would keep a dog.

Having seen Sherlock escape, the dogs who were still inside the crate had become very excited and were now trying to follow. Sherlock could see Pugly's squashed-up nose pushing its way out of the gap. He bent down to help his friend by pulling on Pugly's collar with his teeth.

As soon as Pugly was free, another snout appeared as the large, shaggy dog forced his way through the gap. The planks bent and groaned and finally snapped as the big dog pushed his way out.

Now the other dogs could follow easily. Morrie came next, followed by the two poodles and a completely black dog that Sherlock hadn't even noticed in the dark crate. Last to emerge was the Pekingese, who strolled out through the gap as though it had been opened especially for her.

She glanced around at the dingy surroundings, then sauntered past the other dogs and went to sit on a pile of coiled rope.

The poodles began running around like puppies, excited to be free of the crate, and several of the others lapped greedily at the puddle of water on the floor. Now that they were all out, Sherlock was wondering what they should do next. His thoughts were interrupted by a loud rumbling that ran through all the metal plates of the boat, and a slooshing sound, accompanied by the smell of diesel fumes.

Sherlock had heard that noise and smelled that smell before and he knew what it meant. They were the sounds and smells that boats made when they were starting their engines and preparing to leave. He had to find his way out of here quickly!

With his nose close to the metal decking, he started snuffling his way around the edges of the darkened hold. The other dogs began following closely behind him, snuffling at boxes, poking their noses into corners and pausing occasionally to wee against a crate.

The strange procession moved right around the hold of the ship until they came to a flight of metal steps, leading upwards at a sharp angle. The door at the top was closed but there was a line of clear brightness along the bottom.

Sherlock raised his snout and sniffed at the faint breeze coming from under the door. It smelled of salt air and fish and seagulls and he knew instantly what it meant. On the other side of the door was *the outside*.

Sherlock knew now what he had to do. He threw back his head and let out a great howl that was immediately taken up by all the other dogs. Then he furrowed his brow, lowered his head and charged up the metal stairs. One way or the other, he was going to get past that door.

One way or the other, he was going to get to Charlie.

17

HAPPY REUNION

Charlie stood at the edge of the quayside with her fists clenched. 'This is hopeless!' she cried. 'There are dozens of boats going in and out of this harbour. Sherlock could be on any one of them.'

'It's on account of the tides, see,' said Captain Tom. 'If these boats don't sail now, they'll be stuck here when the current changes.'

'There must be something we can do,' said Max. 'Couldn't the harbour master stop everyone from leaving?'

'Not if the harbour master here is anything like old Creech,' said Joe. 'He wouldn't help us in a million years.' They all remembered the unpleasant

Mr Creech, the harbour master in Southwold, who they had met during their first adventure.

Captain Tom scratched his head. 'Well, I never 'eard of anyone closing a harbour before,' he said. 'But the harbour master here is a good friend of mine. She might help us if she knew it was an emergency. I'll get along and ask her right away.' He hurried away in the direction of a small cabin standing near the harbour entrance.

'That still doesn't help us,' said Charlie. 'The dognappers could be getting away right now.'

'There seems to be something odd going on over there,' said Joe. 'Look!'

They turned to see where Joe was pointing. At the very end of the quayside was an old freighter, smaller than the others and sitting low in the water. The ship's black and green paint was blistered and broken through with streaks of red rust so that it looked like an old, wounded animal.

It looked as though the ship was preparing to leave. Several of the crew were hauling up ropes or carrying boxes up the two long gangplanks at the front and back of the ship, and clouds of blue diesel smoke billowed from the funnel.

What had attracted Joe's attention was the commotion that seemed to have broken out amongst the crew. Several people were running along the deck and a man in a peaked cap was leaning out of the wheelhouse window, pointing and shouting as one of the crew struggled to open a steel door. He pulled frantically at the door's big locking wheel as his colleagues rushed to help.

'They seem to be in a big panic about something,' said Joe.

Charlie took out the binoculars she always carried with her and raised them to her eyes. She could now see two men struggling to open the door while the man in the wheelhouse yelled at them angrily, becoming more red-faced at every moment. As Charlie watched, the men finally unlocked the door and began to haul it open.

Almost immediately, the door exploded

outwards as if a giant spring had been coiled up behind it. The men stumbled backwards onto the deck and stared at the open doorway as something came hurtling from the darkness towards them.

'Dogs!' cried Charlie. 'Lots of dogs.'

'What?' said Max. 'Are you sure?'

'Let me see,' said Lucy. She took the binoculars and squinted through them. There was no mistake: the small freighter was now alive with dogs of all shapes and sizes. They ran wildly up and down the deck, avoiding the grasping hands of the crew, as the sound of distant barking carried on the breeze.

Lucy saw a large poodle leap up at a terrified crewman and pin him to the deck while a yellow Labrador and a Highland terrier chased two men up the main mast and then stood at the bottom, barking furiously as the men clung fearfully to an iron ladder.

The man in the peaked cap, who Lucy thought must be the captain, had now turned bright scarlet with rage. He started down the steps of the wheelhouse with a face like a thundercloud but only got halfway before he met two dogs charging up the stairs towards him. The expression on his face changed to one of terror and he beat a hasty retreat back into the wheelhouse, shutting the door behind him.

'That has to be the boat we're looking for,' cried Lucy. 'There are dogs everywhere.' She focused the binoculars on one of the dogs now barking furiously at the locked wheelhouse door, a scruffy brown and white dog with a barrel chest and floppy ears.

Lucy recognised him at once.

'Sherlock!' she cried. 'Oh, Charlie, I can see Sherlock!'

Charlie grabbed the binoculars back from Lucy, then then she screamed. 'It *is* Sherlock,' she yelled. 'He's still on board the dognappers' boat. Come on, we have to rescue him.' She took off along the quayside at a sprint, closely followed by the others, with Max puffing along at the back.

As they reached the freighter, a large, bearded crewman wearing a panicked expression came lumbering down one of the gangplanks, followed closely by a howling pack of dogs, led by Morrie the Labrador. 'Help me!' shrieked the man when he saw the children. 'They're going eat me!'

He glanced over his shoulder to see Morrie bounding towards him and squealed in terror.

Before Morrie reached him, the big man jumped over the side of the gangplank and dropped five metres into the greasy brown waters below with a noise like a sack of potatoes being dropped into a bath.

The children peered over the edge of the dock to see the big man thrashing around in the water as Morrie scampered up and down the dockside, barking excitedly.

'Help me,' spluttered the man. 'I can't get out.'

Lucy glanced around hurriedly. A short distance away, a bright orange lifebelt hung on a post at the side of the dock. Lucy ran to the post and returned with the belt before dropping it into the water. The big man floundered his way over to the lifebelt and clung on to it, glaring up at them sullenly.

'That was quick thinking,' said Max. 'But what do we do now? Should we call the police?'

Charlie clenched her fists and gritted her teeth. 'Well, *I'm* going on board,' she said. 'My dog's on that ship and *nobody* is going to stop me.'

'We're right with you, Charlie,' said Lucy. 'We'll all go.'

The four children walked towards the gangplank, full of determination. But as they reached the bottom step, they all stopped in their tracks.

Standing proudly at the top of the gangplank was a scruffy dog with short legs and brown patches on his fur. He wore a fierce expression and his floppy ears flowed behind him in the sea breeze.

'Sherlock!'

The word was almost a sob in Charlie's throat. She took two steps forward and then fell to her knees as Sherlock bolted down the plank towards her, barking joyously. The little dog collided with his mistress in an excited ball of wriggling fur, barking and licking and yelping with the sheer delight of being reunited with the girl he loved.

Poor Charlie was so beside herself that, for a long time, all she could do was cover Sherlock in kisses and sob. 'Oh, Sherlock, my darling,' she cried. 'I've been so worried. I'll never let anyone take you away from me again. Not ever!'

Still hugging Sherlock, Charlie turned to her friends, laughing and crying all at the same time. 'It's really him,' she sobbed. 'Come and say hello.'

They all rushed forward and dropped to their knees around Charlie, taking it in turns to hug the wriggling, barking bundle and have their faces thoroughly tongue-washed. It was several minutes before anyone could speak again. Charlie, Lucy and Joe all had tears of joy running down their faces and even Max, who prided himself on being 'a man of science', had a glassy look in his eyes.

'Thank you,' said Charlie. 'Thank you all so much for helping me find my dog. If you hadn't been my friends, then... I might never have seen him again.' Her smile faded for a moment, and she looked down at Sherlock as though she was afraid he might disappear in front of her eyes.

Lucy laid a hand on her friend's shoulder. 'It's okay, Charlie,' she said. 'He's not going anywhere.

And there's no need to thank us; it's what friends are for.'

'Yeah, we're all as pleased to see Sherlock as you are,' said Joe, wiping his eyes. 'Look, even Max is crying.'

They all looked at Max, who frowned very hard and began polishing his glasses on his tie. 'I never cry,' insisted Max, a little too quickly. 'I've just got something in my eye, that's all. It must be this diesel smoke. It really is very bad for the ocular membranes.'

He reached up to dab at a stray tear that was running down his face and then realised that all his friends were grinning at him. 'Oh, alright,' he said with a shrug. 'Perhaps I *do* cry sometimes. But only when something really good happens.' And he reached down and tickled Sherlock behind the ears.

'Look, Captain Tom's coming back,' said Joe, pointing. 'And he's got someone with him.'

Captain Tom was hurrying along the quayside,

accompanied by a stern-looking lady in a peaked cap and a florescent yellow jacket. As they drew closer, Captain Tom gave a gasp of delight. 'You found Sherlock,' he cried. 'Thank heavens for that. Now, if I could only find Pugly.'

No sooner had Tom spoken than there was a delighted bark from behind them and they turned to see a small, cross-eyed dog scampering down the gangplank towards them.

'Pugly!' cried Captain Tom. He scooped up the little dog as Pugly barked and wriggled and licked the captain, making the old man laugh. 'Steady on, old boy. You'll lick my beard right off.'

He turned to the children. 'Thank you for finding my Pugly!' he said. 'If it hadn't been for you, I don't know what I would have done.'

'It's all thanks to Max's artificial nose,' said Charlie.

'But don't make a fuss or he'll start crying again,' said Joe with a grin. 'Oww!' He grimaced as Max jabbed him in the ribs with his elbow.

'Would someone mind telling me what's going

on here?' The stern-faced woman had been looking at all the dogs now running freely up and down the gangplank and at the man still thrashing around in the water. Now she turned to the children and gave them a look that demanded an explanation.

'They're dognappers,' said Joe at once.

'At least some of them are,' said Lucy.

'We followed them here with the artificial nose,' said Max with a grin.

'They stole Sherlock and Pugly too,' said Charlie. 'And all these other dogs must belong to someone as well.'

'It's the Fitchwitheringtons who are behind it all,' said Joe. 'You should find them and arrest them.'

'What I should have done,' said the woman wearily, 'is stay in bed today. I've already had to deal with a report of some jokers trying to jump the bridge on a motorbike.' She gave Captain Tom a narrow look. 'I don't suppose you know anything about that, do you, Tom?'

222

Captain Tom frowned and shook his head vigorously. 'Certainly not, Cathy,' he said, sternly. 'That sounds like very irresponsible behaviour to me.'

The harbour master frowned suspiciously at Tom and then looked down at the man in the water. 'The first thing I need to do is get a police boat over here and get him out of there.' She looked up at the gangplank. 'Then I'm going to have a word with the captain of this vessel.'

She spent a minute talking into the radio pinned to her lapel, then tucked her clipboard under her arm and pulled her cap low over her eyes. 'Right, you lot,' she said. 'Wait here while I go and find out what's going on. No doubt the police will want to talk to you all later.'

They watched her march up the gangplank with a fierce expression. 'I wouldn't want to be the captain of that ship when she gets up there,' said Joe. 'Do you think he's one of the dognappers too?'

Captain Tom shrugged. 'I don't know,' he said. 'The Fitchwitheringtons probably paid him to smuggle the dogs out of the country with no questions asked. Cathy will find out the truth. She doesn't take any nonsense from anyone.'

'Speaking of which,' said Charlie. 'What's happened to the Fitchwitheringtons?'

'Who knows,' said Lucy. 'They're probably miles away by now. It's so awful that they took all your mum's jewellery, Joe.'

'And my laptop,' said Max miserably. 'It will take all my Christmas and birthday money for the next two years before I can get another one.'

'I'm really happy I got Sherlock back,' said Charlie. 'But it seems so unfair that they got away scot-free.'

'Well, someone's getting away,' said Joe. 'Look over there.'

At the rear of the ship, two people were struggling down the smaller gangplank. Even though it was a warm day, both of them were bundled up in thick overcoats with the collars turned up and woolly hats pulled down low over their eyes. They staggered and stumbled under the weight of three large holdalls, as well as a number of overstuffed shopping bags and a suitcase on wheels. When they reached the bottom of the gangplank, they started shuffling away in the other direction.

'Hey!' said Max suddenly. 'That's my backpack!' He pointed at the lead figure, who was wearing a black rucksack slung across his shoulders. Even from here, the children could see that it was covered with *Warlocks and Dragons* stickers. 'Hey, you! Stop, thief!' yelled Max.

The lead figure turned to look at them and they saw very clearly the plump red features of Lord Fitchwitherington staring at them from beneath the woolly hat. When he saw the children, his eyes widened. 'We've been spotted, Maggie,' he yelled.

The second figure turned and they saw it was Lady Fitchwitherington. Beneath her overcoat she wore a long evening dress with high heels and several necklaces draped around her neck. 'It's that Carter brat and his wretched friends,' she shrieked. 'Run for it, Archie!' She began a tottering run along the quayside, closely followed by her husband, who lumbered after her like an overweight bear wearing too many clothes.

'They're getting away,' cried Joe. 'Should we go after them?'

But before anyone could answer, Sherlock took matters into his own paws. He had immediately recognised the voices of Lord and Lady Fitchwitherington from when he was locked inside the crate. He knew these were the people who had taken him away from Charlie and locked him in that horrible place and now he was going to make them pay.

The hackles rose on the back of his neck, and he bared his teeth in a fierce growl. Then he broke away from Charlie's grasp and charged after the couple.

'Sherlock!' cried Charlie. 'Come back, it could be dangerous.'

But Sherlock wasn't listening. He dived through Joe's legs and charged after the escaping couple. When they saw a furious ball of fur bearing down on them, they both shrieked and began to run faster. Several shopping bags dropped to the ground, spilling a long trail of clothes, watches, perfume bottles, phones and jewellery along the dockside in their wake.

Finally, Lady Fitchwitherington dropped the holdalls and the suitcase on wheels. She hitched up her long dress around her skinny white thighs and began to run as fast as she could manage in the high heels. 'It's no good,' cried Lord Fitchwitherington, looking over his shoulder. 'The beast's gaining on us. Quick, over the side.'

He grasped his wife's arm and pulled them both towards the dockside. As Sherlock closed in, barking and snarling, they hesitated for an instant before both leaping into the murky brown waters of the harbour.

The children ran to the spot where Sherlock was now barking ferociously down at the couple as they floundered in the water. 'Do you think we should help them?' said Lucy. 'We don't know if they can swim.'

'I don't think you need to worry,' said Charlie. 'Here's the police boat, look!'

A blue and white motor launch with 'POLICE' on the side surged across the open water towards them. When the launch reached the couple, two hefty policemen leaned over the side and began hauling the wretched Fitchwitheringtons out of the water.

'Well, I'm glad they're okay,' said Lucy. 'Even though they're horrible people.'

'This looks like everything they stole from those houses in Southwold,' said Joe, looking at the various items strung out along the quayside. He picked up a plastic bag and peered inside. 'Hey, this is my mum's jewellery box,' he said pulling it out of the bag. 'I recognise it from her dressing table.'

'And that's my rucksack,' cried Max. He ran to his bag and sat on the ground while he pulled open the zips. 'My laptop's still inside,' he cried, opening the lid. 'And it still works. I'm saved!' He clutched the computer to his chest and beamed.

'Somehow I think the police are going to want to talk to us about all of this,' said Charlie.

'Well, at least no one can blame us this time,' said Joe. 'Everyone's going to be happy when they get their stuff back.'

'Apart from them,' said Max, looking down at the police boat, where the bedraggled Fitchwitheringtons were being wrapped in silver blankets. 'The sooner that whole family are behind bars, the better.'

'Speaking of which,' said Lucy. 'What happened to Miranda? She must be somewhere around here too.'

'Maybe she's still on board,' said Max. 'I'm sure the police will find her.'

'She's not on board the ship,' said Charlie, pointing. 'She's over there, look!'

While they had been preoccupied with the Fitchwitheringtons, they had forgotten all about the gangplank at the front of the boat. A lone figure had crept down the plank and was now a hundred metres away, walking quickly in the direction of the sea front. She wore a black tracksuit and her blonde hair was tucked into a black beanie hat but there was no mistaking her.

It was Miranda Fitchwitherington.

The girl glanced back over her shoulder, and caught sight of them staring at her. Instead of looking surprised or scared, a slow smile crept across her face and she raised a hand in mock salute.

'So long, losers!' she shouted above the noise of the wind. And with that, she turned and broke into a fast, loping run, sprinting away along the quayside. Sherlock growled and lunged after her, but this time Charlie held on firmly to his collar. After the last few days, she was not about to let him anywhere near Miranda Fitchwitherington.

'The police haven't seen her,' wailed Joe, looking down at the police launch. 'She's going to get away.'

'Oh no, she isn't.'

They all turned to Lucy, who was glaring at the retreating figure of Miranda with a deep scowl. None of them could ever remember having seen Lucy look so angry before.

'Lucy?' said Joe, with a worried expression. 'Are you okay?'

'I'm perfectly okay, thanks, Joe,' said Lucy through gritted teeth. She began to remove her tracksuit jacket and her beanie hat and tossed them on the ground.

'Luce?' said Max, nervously. 'W-what are you going to do?'

'I'm going to have a race,' said Lucy in a serious voice. 'And this time, I'm not going to lose. Now, move out of my way.'

And with that, she began to run after Miranda Fitchwitherington.

18

THE SHOWDOWN

Lucy got into her stride quickly.

Any nervousness she had about chasing Miranda Fitchwitherington disappeared quickly as her training kicked in and she imagined her father's voice in her ear. *This is a race, Lucy,* she heard him say. *You need to pace yourself or you will have nothing left at the end.*

She settled into a steady rhythm and focused ahead. Miranda Fitchwitherington was about two hundred metres away, jogging gently along the quayside, seemingly unaware that anyone was following her. Lucy saw that she was nearly at the bridge that marked the end of the harbour. Once

Miranda reached there, she could easily disappear into the surrounding streets or hop on a bus and be lost forever.

She gritted her teeth and picked up her pace. She closed the gap quickly, a hundred metres, eighty, seventy... Some sixth sense must have made Miranda turn and look behind her and she blinked in surprise as she saw the determined figure of Lucy bearing down on her. Then she grinned.

'Well, if it isn't the loser,' she shouted. 'If it's a race you want, Lucy Yeung, then I'll give you one. I've beaten you once and I can do it again.'

Miranda began to sprint away. A group of dockworkers, on their way to work, scattered in surprise as the tall girl ran through their midst. A few moments later, they jumped out of the way again as Lucy flew past, panting with the effort.

Miranda had reached the bridge now and Lucy was beginning to struggle. Her legs burned and her lungs felt like they were on fire. Thinking of her dad, she dug deep inside herself. *You always have more to give than you think you do, Lucy,* he'd say. *Remember that when you're ready to give up.*

She picked up her speed, lengthening her stride and breathing through the pain of a stitch in her side. For a moment she lost sight of Miranda, but as she reached the bridge she saw her again, running across the promenade in front of the pier. She was heading for the seafront.

Miranda's beanie hat flew off in the wind but she didn't stop to pick it up; barely fifty metres separated them now. Lucy's legs trembled with every stride and the sweat ran into her eyes and blurred her vision. She could never remember having run a race this hard before.

Miranda's graceful running style seemed to have deserted her now. She lumbered along the promenade, shoving pedestrians out of the way as she barged her way through. Lucy felt more comfortable now. She trained every day by running along the promenade in Southwold. This was exactly what she was used to.

She refused to let herself slow down; she forced her legs to pump harder as she closed the gap between them... thirty metres, now twenty, now ten.

Now, Lucy, said her dad's voice. *Now is the time for your sprint finish. Give it everything you've got.*

With a superhuman effort, Lucy put on a final burst of speed and, for an instant, all the pain in her legs disappeared and she felt like she was flying. The gap between the two girls closed rapidly. Miranda looked back and panic took hold of her. She veered off the pathway and across a piece of open grass towards a children's playground.

Lucy turned effortlessly, matching the other girl's speed and direction until she was barely an arm's length behind her. She reached out to grab Miranda.

And then she tripped.

She had not seen the child's bicycle on the grass where it had been abandoned by its owner. Her foot caught in one of the wheels and she tumbled forwards.

As she went down, Lucy threw out her arm in

237

desperation and her fingers closed on the other girl's trainer. Lucy's grip was not strong, but it was enough to unbalance Miranda, who fell to the ground.

Lucy did not waste her advantage. She scrambled across the grass and grabbed the other girl firmly around the legs so she could not get up. Miranda Fitchwitherington screamed.

'Get your hands off me, Lucy Yeung,' she shrieked. 'You're a nobody. You're nothing but a loser!' She struggled to get away, but her strength had gone and she couldn't break Lucy's grip.

'That's where you're wrong, Miranda Fitchwitherington,' snarled Lucy. She was vaguely aware of the sound of sirens and of spiralling blue lights somewhere behind them, but she kept her gaze firmly fixed on Miranda. 'Because this time I beat you fair and square. And that makes you the loser!'

A look of cold fury came into Miranda's eyes and for a moment Lucy was genuinely afraid that she might have pushed the girl too far. But then she felt gentle hands pulling her free of the other girl and she turned to find herself looking up at a police officer, who gave her a reassuring smile. 'Well done, miss,' she said kindly. 'You caught her. We were afraid she'd got away.'

Lucy blinked at the police officer in surprise. Nearby, a second officer was pulling Miranda to her feet. 'H-how?' gasped Lucy. 'How did you know where I was?'

The police officer unfolded a crinkly silver blanket from her pocket and draped it around

Lucy's shoulders to keep her warm. 'We arrived at the dockside just after you left,' she said. 'Your friends explained what happened and so we came after you. That was a very brave thing you did.' Then she frowned. 'But it was also very foolish. That could have been extremely dangerous.'

Lucy watched Miranda Fitchwitherington being led away towards the police car. 'I don't care how dangerous it was,' she said quietly. 'I had to chase after her. And I had to beat her.' Then she turned to the officer and smiled. 'Because somebody once told me that winners get to do anything they want.'

19

A FREE DOG
OF THE TOWN

Lucy Yeung made her way along the promenade with a smile on her face. Chasing Miranda Fitchwitherington had been the hardest race of her life and, even though it had happened several days ago, her muscles still ached.

But it had absolutely been worth it. Not only had she stopped Miranda from getting away, she had proved to herself that she could beat her. And now she had some really exciting news that she couldn't wait to share with the others.

She reached the last beach hut in the row and opened the door and was immediately met by a wave of delicious cooking smells. 'Oh wow,' she said, taking off her coat. 'What's Joe cooking up this time?'

'Macaroni cheese,' said Joe proudly. He was standing by the tiny gas cooker, wearing a frilly apron and a pair of oven mitts. 'It's my own recipe, with a special secret ingredient.'

'What's the secret ingredient?' said Lucy.

'Honestly, Luce, if I told you that, it wouldn't be much of a secret now, would it,' said Joe with a frown. 'If the secret got out then anyone could just copy it.'

'It's mustard,' said Max from the corner seat that he always laid claim to. 'I watched him adding it to the sauce earlier. I have to say, though, it tastes amazing.'

'Hey!' complained Joe. 'Not only are you giving away my secret recipe but you've been tasting it behind my back.'

'I couldn't help myself,' said Max innocently. 'You were doing something else, and the pot was right there. You can't leave me alone with food and not expect me to try it; it's against my nature. Anyway, I'm really glad you're here, Luce. Joe said we couldn't have any until you arrived.'

'Well, I'm really pleased to see you too, Max,' said Lucy, taking a seat at the table. 'I must say this looks lovely.'

Joe beamed. The table was laid with a checked tablecloth and a small vase with fresh flowers. There was even a smaller matching cloth on the floor with Sherlock's bowl placed on it. It looked like Joe had gone to a lot of trouble. 'Well, now that we've rescued Sherlock and the beach hut isn't going to be sold, I thought we were all due a celebration,' he said.

'I'm all for celebrations,' said Max. 'Just as long as the food doesn't take too long.'

Lucy looked at Charlie, who was sitting quietly in the other corner, hugging Sherlock and tickling him behind the ears. 'How's Sherlock?' she said. 'Has he got over his ordeal yet?'

Charlie smiled. 'Oh yeah, he got over it as soon as I'd fed him and taken him for a walk.' She bit her lip. 'I'm not sure I have, though. I think it will be a long time before I can trust anyone else to go near him.' She looked up. 'Apart from you guys, I mean. You're all part of Sherlock's family.'

'We're family?' said Max. 'So, me and Sherlock are like brothers? That's so cool. I always wanted a brother who was shorter than I am.'

'Not to mention better-looking,' said Joe.

Everyone laughed as Joe began to dish up platefuls of creamy cheese and macaroni including, as always, a special bowlful just for Sherlock. He immediately buried his snout in the bowl and wolfed it down, then spent several minutes licking cheese sauce from the ends of his whiskers.

'I'm not sure that macaroni is part of a dog's natural diet,' said Charlie with a frown. 'But he loves Joe's cooking so much that I feel mean if I don't let him have it.'

After several minutes, Max pushed back his own bowl with a contented sigh. 'I must say, you've excelled yourself this time, Joseph, old boy,' he said. 'That's quite the best thing you've cooked since the last thing you cooked.'

'I love cooking,' said Joe. 'You should try it sometime. I'm sure you'd like it.'

'Hey,' said Max. 'I have plenty to do taking care of the eating part. Where would the world's great chefs be if it wasn't for people like me? Besides' – he gave them a flash of his eyebrows – 'I have other talents.'

'So apart from eating twice as much as everyone else, what are your other talents?' said Charlie.

'Well, I'm glad you asked me that,' he said importantly. He reached into his backpack and pulled out a thick wodge of newspaper, which he laid on the table. 'Because the headline in this paper says I'm a child genius.'

Lucy looked over his shoulder and her eyes

widened. 'It really does say that,' she sighed. She scanned down the page. 'It goes on and on about how he invented an artificial nose to catch the dognappers.'

Joe rolled his eyes. 'Not again,' he said. 'He'll be unsufferable for a week.'

'Get this,' said Lucy, 'there's even a quote from him here.' She cleared her throat. '"When asked the secret of his success as a detective, Maximillian Green replied, 'When you have eliminated the impossible, whatever remains, however improbable, must be the truth.'" Max, I can't believe you quoted Sherlock Holmes!'

Max grinned. 'Yeah, I was particularly proud of that bit,' he said. 'Don't worry, it mentions you guys too. Somewhere down at the bottom.'

'Here it is,' said Lucy, running her finger down the column. 'It says, "a gang of notorious burglars were caught thanks to the efforts of the After-School Detective Club, a group of heroic young sleuths who have solved several mysteries in the Southwold area".'

'So, you see, we're all famous again,' said Max. 'I can see I'm going to have to make another YouTube video for our fans.'

'My nan thought the last one was great,' said Joe. 'Mind you, I think she was the only one who watched it.'

'This bit's interesting,' said Charlie. 'It says here that the Fitchwitheringtons aren't a real lord and lady at all. Their real names are Archie and Maggie Fitch and they're wanted in four different counties for burglary and fraud. Apparently, they travel all over the country getting estate agents to show them around houses before they burgle them.'

'Poor Mum,' said Joe. 'She really did think she was going to sell them a big house and become employee of the month.'

'What about Miranda?' said Joe. 'Where does she fit in?'

Charlie continued reading. 'It says that when

he wasn't burgling houses, Archie Fitch would drive around with his daughter looking for dogs that they could snatch off the street. She would jump out and put them in the boot of the Bentley and they'd drive off before the owner spotted them.'

'What horrible people,' said Lucy.

'There's more here about Miranda,' said Charlie. 'It also says that she's a lot older than she looks. In fact, she shouldn't have even been in our school at all.'

'So why was she there?' said Max, puzzled.

'It was all part of the plan,' said Charlie. 'Apparently, the Fitches enrolled her in the junior school so she could make friends with the local kids and find out which families had anything worth stealing. Can you believe that?'

Joe frowned. 'So, if she was older than the rest of us then she shouldn't have been competing in our school sports day. Her race against Lucy was unfair.'

'That's what I've been waiting to tell you all,' said Lucy excitedly. 'The school called just before I came out. They said they'd just found out how old Miranda really was and so they've disqualified her. So that means that I was the winner after all.'

'That's great Luce,' said Max. 'But it's just a pity you didn't get to be the winner on the day.'

Lucy beamed from ear to ear. 'I'm not worried about that,' she said. 'Because I won the race, it means I get to try out for the county athletics squad after all. It means I'm on my way to becoming an Olympic athlete.'

The others stared at her for a moment and then erupted into shouting and cheering. Charlie embraced Lucy while Joe and Max pounded each other with cushions. Poor Sherlock was startled awake from a macaroni-induced sleep and blinked at them all curiously before wagging his tail and joining in with a cheerful bark.

'Luce, that's the best news ever,' said Max when they had all calmed down. 'How about we all walk up to the pier for ice cream to celebrate, my treat.'

'Seriously?' said Joe. 'You want to eat ice cream after two helpings of macaroni?'

'Two helpings of macaroni and an ice cream is a perfectly balanced three-course meal, Joseph. You should know that by now.'

'Can anyone else hear something?' said Charlie. 'It sounds like barking outside.' She frowned. 'Maybe we should go and check. Somebody might be in trouble.'

'Don't look so worried,' said Lucy. 'It's probably nothing.'

'Yeah, there aren't any more dognappers in Southwold,' said Joe. 'We made them extinct.'

There was a sudden knock on the door and they looked up to see a familiar figure on the other side of the glass. 'It's Captain Tom,' said Joe.

They opened the door to greet Tom and made a big fuss of Pugly, who was scampering around his feet. 'Come in, Captain Tom,' said Joe. 'We've still got some macaroni left.'

'Oh, er... no thanks, young Joe,' said the captain. 'I've just had me lunch. I've been sent to ask if you wouldn't mind stepping outside for a moment. There's some people out here who'd like a word with you.'

The captain's face looked so serious that they were all immediately worried. 'Who wants to speak to us?' said Lucy.

'It's not the police again, is it?' said Joe. 'We went over our story with them loads of times already.'

'Don't tell me someone else has lost a dog,' said Max. 'There's only so much geniusing I can do in a week.'

Captain Tom raised his hands. 'No, no, it ain't nothing like that,' he said. 'Best you come outside and see for yourselves.'

Feeling more curious by the moment, they followed Tom onto the veranda of the beach hut. As they stepped through the door, someone called out, 'Here they come,' and a cheer went up.

The four children and Sherlock blinked in surprise.

Gathered on the sandy beach were dozens of people, each one of them accompanied by a dog. There were big dogs, little dogs, brown dogs, black dogs, well-behaved and naughty dogs and tiny dogs with fooffed-up hair with ribbons in it.

They recognised Mr Pickering from the amusement arcade with his dog, Morrie, and Sanjay the plumber with Jasmine. A young couple held on to two identical poodles and a girl about their own age was holding a shaggy dog that was larger than she was.

It looked like every dog in Southwold was there.

Max nudged Joe in the ribs. 'What's going on?' he hissed out of the corner of his mouth.

'I dunno,' whispered back Joe. 'Perhaps we're in trouble. Hang on, something's happening.'

Captain Tom held up a hand for silence and cleared his throat noisily. 'Er... unaccustomed as I am to public speaking,' he began, 'that is, er, what I mean to say is, I am humbled and... er, honoured to be present at this most important occasion... er...' He paused and scratched his head.

'What's he saying?' said Charlie.

'We're definitely in trouble,' said Joe. 'I can always tell.'

'Well, you've had a lot of practice,' whispered Max.

Captain Tom was becoming more and more muddled and several people were now looking distinctly confused. 'What I'm trying to say,' he said with a frown, 'is we would all like to extend our greetings and felicitations to our... noble and esteemed... er. Oh 'eck, I'm no good at this public speaking!'

'Perhaps I should take over from here, Thomas?' announced a shrill voice.

Standing at the front of the group was a fat lady wearing a feathered hat and a purple coat. There was a heavy gold chain around her neck, on which hung a large coat of arms. Two men in business suits stood either side of her, looking very official, and they stepped forward to help her up the three steps to the veranda.

Captain Tom looked immensely relieved. He

smiled gratefully and touched the peak of his cap. 'Thank you, Cornelia,' he said. 'I think you're probably much better at this than me.'

The fat woman waited patiently while Tom stepped down to join the others on the beach. Now that she was standing next to them, the children could see she was holding the Pekingese they had last seen on board the ship. The little dog looked much cleaner now. Its fur had been neatly combed and there were fresh ribbons in its hair, but it still had a spiteful look in its eye, and it glared at them angrily.

'Thank you, Mr Crofford,' said the woman. 'My name is Cornelia Jobsworthy, Mayor of Southwold,' she announced. 'And I am here today because we all wish to extend our gratitude to these young people and their stout-hearted little dog, for their bravery in rescuing our four-legged friends from those villainous dognappers.'

Cornelia Jobsworthy paused and smiled while the crowd applauded politely.

'Good news, Joe,' whispered Max. 'I don't think we're in trouble.'

Captain Tom gave them a broad wink. 'Cornelia's so much better at this than me,' he said. 'I guess it goes with her job.'

Cornelia Jobsworthy held her hand up for silence. 'If these valiant youngsters hadn't rescued my beloved Fru-Fru, then I dread to think what might have happened to her.'

She hugged Fru-Fru more tightly and the Pekingese growled to show her displeasure. Cornelia Jobsworthy continued as though she hadn't noticed. 'So, by the powers vested in me as mayor, it is with great pleasure that I hereby award these brave children the Freedom of the Town of Southwold. Mr Benson, if you please.' One of the two suited men stepped forward, bearing a small box.

Joe's eyes had turned round with amazement. 'Did she say we had the freedom of the town?' he said. 'That's brilliant. I'm going to eat all the ice cream in the pier shop.'

'I don't think it means you're free to do anything you want, Joe,' said Lucy.

'Indeed not, young man,' said Cornelia Jobsworthy. 'The Freedom of the Town is an honorary title, given to people who have done great service for the town. You are being given this award to celebrate your valour and cunning in apprehending the dognappers.'

She reached into the box and pulled out a small ribbon decorated with a smaller version of the town crest, and pinned it to Lucy's jacket. Then she fetched three more ribbons and pinned them to Max, Joe and Charlie. 'Congratulations, my dears,' she said when she was finished. 'You were all extremely brave.'

There was another round of polite applause and a man from the local paper took some photographs. Then Cornelia Jobsworthy insisted on giving each of them a hug, which meant they either had their noses squashed against her chain of office or they were snapped at by Fru-Fru.

Then the mayor called for silence once more. 'I have one more official duty to perform today,' she said. 'It is said that a dog is a man's best friend. Well, there is one particular dog here today who is not only the best friend of man but also of all the other dogs in the town.' She looked down at Sherlock and smiled. 'This brave little dog single-handedly led all his friends to freedom. Without him, this story would have ended very differently. And so, it is with great pleasure that I make Sherlock the first ever Free Dog of the Town.'

Cornelia Jobsworthy reached into the box for a final time and held up a small medal on a loop of ribbon. Then she turned to Charlie. 'Miss Wells, if you please?'

Charlie quickly bent down and picked up Sherlock so that Cornelia Jobsworthy could hang the ribbon around his neck while Fru-Fru looked on jealously. When the mayor had finished,

Charlie held up a very confused-looking Sherlock so that everyone could see him.

Cheers erupted from the crowd and all the dogs in the group began barking at the same time. Sherlock seemed to get the idea that they were cheering him and also began barking excitedly in Charlie's arms.

As the cheering died down, the photographer moved in again to take more pictures. 'Perhaps I could get one of you hugging Sherlock, Madam Mayor?' suggested the photographer. 'Our readers would like that.'

The mayor leaned in close to Sherlock and patted him affectionately on the head. Unfortunately, having watched her mistress heap praise on another dog, this final act proved to be more than Fru-Fru could bear. As the mayor leaned in closer, the jealous Pekingese reached out and bit the end of Sherlock's tail. Poor Sherlock yelped in surprise and turned furiously on his attacker.

Almost at once, Fru-Fru, realised she had made

a terrible mistake. She scrambled frantically out of Cornelia Jobsworthy's arms and scurried down the steps to the beach like a frightened rat. 'Fru-Fru, my baby,' cried Cornelia Jobsworthy. 'My darling is escaping. Somebody stop her!'

Sherlock watched Fru-Fru escape through the legs of the crowd and, before Charlie could stop him, he leaped out of her grasp and dashed after the little Pekingese, barking ferociously.

'Sherlock!' yelled Charlie. 'You bad dog! Come back here, at once!'

Charlie took off after Sherlock, scattering the crowd as she pursued him along the beach. She was closely followed by a wailing Cornelia Jobsworthy, frantic for the safety of Fru-Fru and, lastly, by the photographer, who had realised that a good story was developing and was delightedly snapping pictures.

The crowd cheered at the sight of the chase and the two men in business suits looked at each other guiltily, uncertain about whether they should go and help the mayor. As the crowd began to drift away, Lucy, Max and Joe exchanged guilty glances.

'Well,' said Max finally. 'I guess that's the end of our Freedom of the Town.'

'Yeah,' said Joe. 'We're definitely in trouble this time.'

They paused to watch Charlie running up the beach, bright red in the face and yelling furiously at Sherlock as he bolted after Fru-Fru. Then Lucy smiled. 'I don't care if we get into trouble,' she said. 'I'm just really pleased that Charlie and Sherlock are back to their normal selves again.'

And the three friends laughed, then went back inside the beach hut and closed the door.

Don't miss the other books in
The After-School Detective Club series!
Here's what other readers have to say . . .

'The Case of the Smuggler's Curse gets a 10/10
from me... and a double thumbs up! I loved that it
is a modern day mystery and it had me gripped –
I could never have predicted the ending! It felt like
all of the characters could be my friends, especially
Lucy and I pictured hanging out with her, plotting
ideas in the beach hut. I felt like I was there with them!
I really hope to have a whole shelf of After School
Detective Club books one day and can't wait to
find out what else they might get up to!'

By Tabitha, age 8

'Southwold, smugglers and a dog called Sherlock:
this book has everything! It's about four children who
go on an adventure and stop a notorious smuggling ring,
and I think it's absolutely fantastic. There were twists,
turns and surprises around every corner, and that
made it a thrill to read.'

By Imogen, age 12

'I found this an exciting fast-moving story and
I always wanted to read another chapter even
when it was time for bed!'

By Lizzie, age 7

'I would recommend this book to everybody in the world! It's so good, I could marry it! It's packed with adventure, determination, and courage.'

By Sam, age 8

'This gripping story is about four children who meet by coincidence and become firm friends, despite many differences. The children are not perfect, they have quirky personalities, but it makes them relatable. My favourite character is Charlie; she appears fierce, but is also warm-hearted as she loves her dog Sherlock.'

By Akshay, age 9

'I love this book so much. It has a lot of twists, which really surprised me, in a good way.

My favourite character is Charlie because she will stop at nothing to protect her friends and dog. She has a huge personality. She is very independent, she loves dogs, and she is feisty, just like me!'

By Jasmine, age 9

'The Case of the Smuggler's Curse is the best book I've ever read. It contains everything that excites me about reading, I wish I was a part of it! I particularly enjoyed the mixture of adventure, happiness and some sadness. I loved the cliff-hangers; they made me want to read on.'

By Rosie, age 10

'The After School Detective Club is a great book series!
My favourite one is The Secret of Ragnar's Gold.
It's about the After School Detective Club staying at a
spooky castle. It's full of fun, adventure and cliffhangers.
I read it with my dad and loved it!'

By Katee, age 10

'This book is amazing you should definitely
read it one day. It is about a group of children that
meet on the beach and see someone signalling
whom they suspect is a smuggler. That is the start
of the mysterious adventure. I think if you have
never been to Southwold before this will make
you really want to go. I could imagine being in
this adventure story myself. It is very exhilarating
but it would be really scary in real life.'

By Sophie, age 8

'This is a very exciting story about a group
of four kids, Lucy, Max, Joe, Charlie and Sherlock
the dog. They all become friends whilst solving
a mystery about smugglers in their seaside town.
Sherlock was my favourite as he wasn't afraid
of the bad guys and always protected his owner,
Charlie. Sometimes I imagine being a detective
and having a dog like Sherlock. I would call
him Scooby and we would solve mysteries
together after school and at weekends.'

By Freddie, age 10

The After-School Detective Club

The After-School Detective Club are back in
The Legend of the Headless Horseman.

Read on for a preview of the opening chapter . . .

1

THE TREAT

'You've done what?' Charlie Wells stopped what she was doing and glared angrily at her mother, Brenda.

Brenda Wells took a deep breath before continuing. She had learned from bitter experience that arguments with Charlie rarely went well. 'Don't snap at me that way, Charlie,' she sighed. 'I just said I thought it would be nice if we spent some time together this summer so I've arranged a little treat for us. Now pass me the hammer.'

They were standing in the tiny back garden of their house in Southwold. Brenda was at the top of a rickety stepladder while Charlie stood at the bottom holding it steady. This was a difficult task because the ladder was very small, and Brenda was very large and it was all Charlie could do to stop her toppling into the compost heap.

'What kind of treat?' said Charlie suspiciously as she handed her mother the hammer. She knew Brenda's idea of things they 'could do together' usually involved classes in how to tie-dye your old T-shirts or bake wholemeal bread hard enough to break your teeth.

'It's something we'll both enjoy,' said her mother. 'Now don't talk to me for a minute, I need to focus.' She frowned in concentration as she reached up into the apple tree and hammered in a nail. Then she picked up a tangle of fishing line and scrap metal and draped it over the nail, where it jangled tunelessly.

'What is that thing, anyway?' said Charlie.

Brenda leaned back and admired her handiwork. 'It's a wind chime,' said Brenda.

'Miriam makes them from old tin cans she finds on the beach. It will attract healing energies to my meditation space.'

Charlie looked up at the clanking metal shapes. 'It'll frighten the birds away from my bird table,' she said.

'Well, I think it's a beautiful,' said Brenda coming down the ladder. 'Look, even Sherlock agrees.'

Sherlock was curled up on the grass in a patch of sunshine. When he heard his name, he raised his head, scratched behind his ear with a back leg, yawned and then went back to sleep.

'I've seen him more enthusiastic about going to the vets,' said Charlie. 'So, tell me about this treat.'

Brenda sat on the bottom step of the ladder and placed her hands on her lap. 'Well,' she said with obvious excitement. 'Do you remember that yoga teacher I told you about, Guru Pantalooni?'

Charlie frowned. 'You mean the guy who's

on the cover of your yoga magazine?' Brenda owned a large number of books, magazines and DVDs on the subject of yoga, that were filled with pictures of people pulling their arms and legs into impossible positions. The cover of this month's edition featured a round man with red hair, sitting with his eyes closed in a cross-legged position.

'That's him,' said Brenda. 'Well, Miriam bought a ticket for one of his courses but now she can't go so she's offered it to me, isn't that wonderful?'

Charlie could not see anything remotely wonderful about it. 'Yoga? You know I can't stand yoga. Putting your foot behind your head just isn't natural.'

Brenda frowned. 'The ticket is for me, silly. But I thought you might like to come along so we could spend some time together.'

Charlie frowned. 'Why would I want to spend time watching you do yoga in a dusty church hall?'

Brenda rolled her eyes. 'No, Charlie, you're not listening. The course isn't in the church hall, it's at Guru Pantalooni's yoga school in Ireland.'

'Ireland?' said Charlie. 'You can't go all the way to Ireland just for one yoga class.'

'It's not just one class, silly, it's a three-day course,' said her mother. 'I've checked online and we can get cheap flights and hire a little car while we're there. And the best part is, I've rented us a cottage right out in the countryside in a lovely little place called 'Gleann na Sióg'. I think it's Irish but I don't know what it means. Honestly, Charlie, it will be like a little holiday for both of us.'

Charlie groaned. 'What am I supposed to do all by myself while you're off doing yoga?' she complained.

Brenda frowned. 'Just do what you normally do, Charlie,' she said. 'Go for long walks and spot birds. You're always saying how much you love the countryside.'

'We live in Southwold, Mum,' said Charlie. 'I'm already in the countryside. Besides, it's the start of the summer holidays and I want to be with my friends. Can't I just stay here while you go?'

Brenda looked at her feet uncomfortably. 'Ah, well, that might not be so easy,' she said.

'Why not?'

'Well, the thing is,' said Brenda with a pained expression. 'The trip worked out quite expensive so the only way I could afford it was to rent out our house while we're away.'

Charlie's jaw dropped open. 'You rented this place?' She looked up at the house with its peeling paint and leaky gutters and the weeds that sprouted thickly between the patio slabs. 'You mean someone actually wants to stay in this dump?'

Brenda looked hurt. 'Don't be like that. You'd be surprised how many people want a house by the seaside for a few days.' She stood up and began to fold up the step ladder. 'Anyway, it's all arranged now, so you'll have to come with me whether you like it or not.'

Charlie took a deep breath and counted to ten. She had promised herself that she would try and get on better with her mum, and Brenda really seemed to want to go on this yoga course. 'Alright,' she said eventually. 'I'll come with you. I suppose me and Sherlock can always go for some nice walks.'

Brenda started to look uncomfortable again. 'Ah, well, about that,' she said, as she busied herself putting the hammer and nails back in the toolbox. 'The people who rented the cottage were very specific that no pets were allowed. I'm afraid Sherlock can't come with us.'

'What do you mean, he can't come with us?' gasped Charlie. 'Where else is he going to go?'

'He'll have to go to the kennels for a few days,' said Brenda. 'Don't look so worried, darling. Lots of people put their dogs in kennels while they go on holiday.'

Charlie's face had turned white with anger. 'While I don't! I can't be apart from Sherlock. Not even for a few days.'

Since their last adventure when Sherlock had been stolen by dognappers, Charlie could not bear to be parted from him, even for an hour. So, the prospect of going away without him was more than she could bear.

Now it was Brenda's turn to look cross. 'Honestly, Charlie, I never heard anyone make so much fuss about going on holiday.' She slammed the toolbox lid shut. 'Well, I'm afraid it's all arranged. You and I are going to go to Ireland and Sherlock's going into the kennels and that's all there is to it.'

Charlie scowled. 'Well thanks for asking what I wanted, Mum,' she snapped. 'This is going to be the worst summer holidays ever. Come on, Sherlock.'

Charlie turned on her heel and stomped away with Sherlock following close behind.

She slammed the back door so hard that Miriam's wind chime fell out of the tree and hit the ground with a dull clang.

'Oh dear,' said Brenda. 'That really didn't go very well at all.'